NIGHT IN GOA

SURYA SAXENA

Made with ♥ on the Notion Press Platform
www.notionpress.com

I dedicate this book to my friends,
Vijay Gurjar, Shubham Sharma, Avnish Chhabra, and
Kartik Prajapati.

Your camaraderie and spirit have inspired every twist and
turn of this tale.
Thank you for being a part of my journey, both in fiction
and in life.

Contents

About The Book

Have you ever felt like your daily routine lacks excitement, leaving you drained and yearning for something more? Sometimes, the monotony of work and life's responsibilities can build up, making you crave an escape—a break to recharge your mind and spirit. In moments like these, what would you choose? A peaceful vacation to unwind, reconnecting with friends, or perhaps combining both by taking a trip with your closest pals? Such an adventure could be just the refreshment you need, a perfect way to regain your energy and perspective.

But what if that much-needed getaway turned into something far from relaxing—a trip so unforgettable, it leaves an indelible mark on your memory for entirely unexpected reasons?

This is the story of four friends seeking a break from their mundane lives, eager to create memories of laughter and adventure. Little do they know, their journey will plunge them into a whirlwind of unforeseen chaos and challenges. From embarking on their trip with carefree excitement to confronting trials that test their courage and friendship, this tale is a rollercoaster of fun, fear, and survival.

Preface

In a group of friends, the origin of your friendship may not hold much significance compared to the memories you create together. While you may have started your journey together, there may come a time when you and your loved ones get separated. The crucial aspect lies in how you nurture and cherish that friendship, regardless of the physical distance or time apart.

The true value of friendship shines through when you find yourself in a situation where you have no one but a single friend by your side, supporting you unwaveringly. It is during these moments that you realize the depth of your bond and the importance of having someone who has your back.

Regardless of how much time passes, whether it be days, months, or even years, the key lies in how you reconnect and interact with your friend when you cross paths again. The way you welcome each other and the genuine connection you share is what truly matters. It is a testament to the strength of your friendship and whether you have grown together or remained true to yourselves throughout the journey.

In this story, there are four boys named Bunny, Vijay, Shubham (Shubh), and Avnish (Avi), who yearn to break free from their mundane lives and experience some excitement. They find themselves caught in the monotonous routine of their respective jobs.

Bunny and Vijay are colleagues in a corporate company, leading a similar life of working long hours from 9 to 7 every day. They are based in Bangalore, both in their twenties, and feel stuck in the daily grind of following orders from their managers and going to the office.

Shubham, known as Shubh to his friends, works for a sales company. His job involves traveling to different places regularly, never settling in one location for long.

Lastly, Avnish, also known as Avi, is an entrepreneur running his own business in his hometown.

Despite their busy schedules and lack of simultaneous free time, the four friends are determined to reunite and go on an adventure together. Faced with the challenge of conflicting schedules, they decide to embark on a spontaneous and unplanned trip.

As their journey unfolds, they encounter various experiences that leave a profound impact on their lives. It becomes a transformative journey where they witness new places, meet different people, and engage in adventures that change their perspectives and outlook on life forever.

Throughout the trip, their bond strengthens, and they realize the value of friendship and the importance of seizing moments of joy amidst the monotony of their daily routines. The trip becomes a turning point, awakening their desire for more meaningful and fulfilling lives beyond their regular work.

The story explores the unfolding events of their trip, the unexpected encounters, and the personal growth they undergo, ultimately leading to a deeper appreciation for life and their friendship.

About The Author

Surya Saxena, a 25-year-old dreamer and storyteller, crafts tales that blend the vividness of real life with the allure of fiction. Living in a world where imagination knows no bounds, Surya finds inspiration in the mundane, the extraordinary, and the mysterious. His passion for weaving narratives comes alive in his book, which features a collection of gripping story, each with its own unique flavor and depth.

One of the standout tales in this collection is A Night in Goa, After the success of "Let's Fall In Love" he came back with a dark thriller that plunges readers into a world of danger, betrayal, and unexpected twists. Drawing inspiration from both personal experiences and boundless creativity, Surya creates a story that feels hauntingly real yet delightfully unsettling. Set against the vibrant yet shadowy backdrop of Goa's nightlife, the tale follows a group of friends whose seemingly fun vacation turns into a harrowing descent into chaos. With a perfect balance of psychological thrills, gore, and dark humor, A Night in Goa showcases Surya's knack for storytelling that leaves readers on the edge of their seats.

Surya's writing reflects his belief that every story has the power to transport its readers—to make them laugh, cry, or shiver with anticipation. He strives to explore the complexities of human emotions and relationships, often blurring the line between reality and fiction.

When he's not writing, Surya can be found exploring new places, observing life, and collecting experiences that might one day become the foundation for his next great story. With this book, he invites readers to step into his world of dreams and stories—where anything is possible, and nothing is ever as it seems.

A Book By

Penaaki

CHAPTER ONE

TRAPPED IN THE LOOP

Bunny was the kind of guy who thrived on fun—late-night parties, spontaneous adventures, and endless banter with his friends. But ever since he joined an EdTech company, his life had taken a drastic turn. The once carefree Bunny now found himself stuck in a suffocating 9-to-5 routine. Work deadlines replaced his weekend plans, and the only time he saw his friends was in his memories.

The one silver lining in his office life was Vijay, a teammate who shared his misery. Vijay was a workaholic who excelled in everything, which often made Bunny wonder if Vijay had secretly signed a deal with the corporate devil.

It wasn't long before Bunny introduced Vijay to his old friends, Shubh and Avi, and the four quickly bonded. But their growing friendship didn't ease Bunny's frustration with his monotonous life. Each morning began with the same ritual: wake up, go to work, survive the manager's wrath, and crawl back home.

One fine day, Vijay and Bunny were getting ready for work.

Vijay: (adjusting his tie) "Hey, bro, I don't have a good feeling about today."

Bunny: "Why is it that whenever you say something, it's like a prophecy of doom?"

Vijay: "I don't know, man. It's just a feeling."

Bunny: "Yeah, and the last time you had one of these 'feelings,' we ended up stuck in an all-day meeting with that sadist manager. Thanks for that."

Vijay: "Hey, don't blame me. I'm not responsible for your bad luck."

Bunny: "You're the harbinger of my bad luck. Stop predicting disasters, will you?"

They trudged to the office, where their worst fears came true.

Vijay had a girlfriend in the office and they both used to behave like they didn't know each other. Vijay really loved his girlfriend. But his girlfriend was very demanding and wanted to have control over Vijay's life. She doesn't let him smoke or drink or spend time with his friends.

As soon as they arrived, their manager pounced on them like a lion on wounded prey.

Morning sync-up started. Vijay and Bunny got new projects to work on. Their time was already booked with the work they are already doing. Now they have more work to do and now they don't have time for anything else. Manager used to scold Bunny everyday. If he makes a small mistake in his work then Manager just comes and scolds him on a regular basis. Bunny just wanted to get out of this loop of a 9 to 5 job and wanted to enjoy his life so that he can feel that he is alive. But this life did not give him any chances to do so.

Manager: "Bunny, how many times do I have to repeat myself? This report is a disaster!"

Bunny: (muttering under his breath) "Well, so is my life, but you don't see me yelling about it."

Manager: "What was that?"

Bunny: (forcing a smile) "Nothing, sir! I'll fix it immediately."

Meanwhile, Vijay sat at his desk, pretending not to notice Bunny's torment.

Bunny: "You know what, Vijay? I think our manager is actually Satan in disguise."

Vijay: "You mean he's not?"

Bunny: "I bet he feeds on our misery to stay alive. Every time he yells at me, I feel like a piece of my soul dies, and he grows another hair on his bald head."

Vijay: "Well, at least he's consistent."

By noon, their workload had doubled thanks to another round of surprise projects. Bunny leaned back in his chair, staring at the ceiling.

Bunny: "You ever feel like a hamster on a wheel, Vijay?"

Vijay: "Every day, bro. But at least the hamster has snacks."

While Bunny was battling corporate hell, Shubh was battling his own demons. His job required him to travel between cities and states, closing deals and meeting clients. Each day brought new challenges, and Shubh often joked that he was singlehandedly keeping the travel industry alive.

On the other hand, Avi lived life on his own terms. He ran his business like a king, taking vacations whenever he pleased and working only when the mood struck him. But even Avi wasn't immune to frustration. But he was doing this all alone and he wanted to go out with his friends and wanted to enjoy his life with his friends

Avi: (to himself) "What's the point of freedom if you've got no one to share it with?"

They all were frustrated with their life. They wanted to get out of the loop of the life they were living in and the illusion they were living in. They want to break it and feel something different, something new.

Vijay and Bunny reached their room after office. They both were not happy.

Bunny: (throwing his bag on the floor) "I'm so done, bro! I can't handle this anymore. It's like a never-ending nightmare."

Vijay: "What's got you all worked up now?"

Bunny: "We work ourselves to death every day, and for what? A paycheck that barely covers rent and therapy?"

Vijay: Speak for yourself, buddy. My life is sorted.

Bunny: "Oh, really? You're happy being a corporate zombie? Aspiring to win the 'Employee of the Month' tombstone?"

Vijay: "Better than being the 'Most Complained About Employee.'"

Bunny: Oh, really? Please tell me, what's so sorted about being trapped in this corporate circus?

Vijay: Well, you see, I aspire to be a professional slave. It's my calling!

Bunny: Are you serious? That's the dumbest and most absurd thing I've heard today.

Vijay: Whatever, man.

Bunny: You don't understand! The manager only targets me, scolding me for the tiniest mistakes.

Vijay: Maybe it's because you make those mistakes all the time.

Bunny: Oh, please!

Vijay: Look, bro, face the reality. You can't escape your cubicle and the office drama. So, what's the point in complaining?

Bunny: Just shut the hell up, Vijay!

Frustrated, Bunny called Avi for some much-needed relief.

Bunny: Hey, man, what's up?

Avi: Yo, bro! What's going down?

Bunny: "Life sucks."

Avi: "Tell me something new. Corporate crap, huh?"

Bunny: Everything feels like it's falling apart, man. Corporate life is sucking the life out of me.

Avi: Ah, the good ol' corporate shit. I've been telling you, my friend, you need a break from that madness.

Bunny: Yeah, I know, but it feels impossible to break free.

Avi: Well, here's the plan: let's go on a hilarious adventure. You, me, Shubh, and even Vijay.

Bunny: "Yeah. I need a break, dude. A long one."

Avi: "Then let's make it happen. You, me, Shubh, and Vijay—Goa this weekend. No excuses."

Bunny: "Goa? How am I supposed to convince Vijay and Shubh? Vijay won't leave his cubicle, and Shubh is probably halfway across the country."

Avi: That's the challenge. Meet me at the Goa Airport on Saturday morning with Vijay. I'll handle Shubh.

Bunny: But how am I supposed to convince Vijay?

Bunny: "This is madness."

Avi: "No, this is Goa, my friend. See you Saturday morning."

For the first time in weeks, Bunny felt a spark of excitement.

Avi: Do whatever it takes, man. Get creative! We'll be waiting for you.

Bunny: Got it! We'll make it happen.

Avi: That's the spirit! See you soon,

Now Bunny is filled with excitement and a mischievous determination to make this trip a reality. He knows he can't ask Vijay or Shubh directly, or they'll probably decline. But with Avi's help, Bunny is ready to embark on a hilarious journey, bracing himself for the comedic challenges ahead.

Bunny: (to Vijay) "Pack your bags, buddy. We're going to Goa."

Vijay: "Over my dead body."

Bunny: (grinning) "If that's what it takes."

CHAPTER TWO

THE ROAD TO GOA

Avi, determined to recruit Shubh for the trip, marched straight to his place the next day. If persuasion didn't work, he was prepared to resort to morally questionable methods.

Avi: "Bro, don't you miss the good ol' days? Wild parties, crazy adventures, zero responsibilities?!"

Shubh: What are you talking about? Have you lost your mind? Are you high?

Avi: No, no! I mean, don't you miss the epic adventures, the wild parties, the carefree days? We need to relive those moments, man!

Shubh: Yeah, I do miss all that, but you know how it is. Nobody has any time these days.

Avi: But don't you have time? You work only half the week, and the other half, you're just chilling at home or jet-setting around.

Shubh: I travel to build connections and seal deals, my friend.

Avi: That's true, but can't you spare a day or two for old times' sake?

Shubh: What's the point you're trying to make here?

Avi leaned in, grinning like a cat that just cornered a mouse.

Avi: "We're going to Goa. This week. Me, you, Bunny, and Vijay. It's going to be legendary."

Shubh: (laughing nervously) "Goa? Are you out of your mind? I can't just take off. I've got a job, a girlfriend's dad to impress, and a wedding to save for. If I slack off, he'll marry her off to some rich idiot who drives a BMW."

Avi smirked, playing his trump card.

Avi: Ah, but if you don't come with us, I might just accidentally let slip what happened at our last wild party. You remember, right?

Shubh: Are you freaking blackmailing me now?

Avi: Well, it seems like it, my friend. So, what's it gonna be? An unforgettable trip with us or the risk of your love interest discovering your party shenanigans?

Shubh: You're insane, but fine! I'll do it. But remember, if anything goes wrong, I'm blaming you!

Avi: (grinning) "Deal. Welcome to the wild side, my friend. My adventurous comrade! Get ready for the wildest time of your life! We will have fun."

On the other side of the country.....

Back in Bangalore, Bunny was cooking up his own plan to rope Vijay into the trip. The office monotony had reached unbearable levels, and Bunny wasn't about to let Vijay's overbearing girlfriend ruin his shot at freedom.

One fine Friday,

Bunny and Vijay found themselves sitting next to each other in the office, going about their usual work routine. However, Bunny couldn't contain his boredom any longer and decided to approach Vijay with an idea.

Bunny: "Bro, I can't do this anymore. This cubicle life is killing me. We need to do something fun!"

Vijay: (rolling his eyes) "Fun? You're kidding, right?"

Bunny: Bro... this is getting so monotonous, man. We haven't done anything fun in ages.

Vijay: What are you even talking about?

Bunny: "No! I mean it. Let's hit the bar tonight, have a few drinks, and plan something crazy."

Vijay: No, I can't.

Bunny: Why not?

Vijay: You know I have too many responsibilities. I can't take time off or go anywhere.

Bunny: Come on, bro! Today is Friday. Let's have a few drinks tonight, and we have tomorrow off. It'll be a blast!

Vijay: No, you don't understand. You know how she is. (Referring to his girlfriend)

Bunny: Oh, shut the f up, man! It's like she wears the pants in the relationship, and you just bend over every night!

Vijay: Stop it! That's not true.

Bunny: But it is! I can prove it.

Vijay: It doesn't matter. Your tricks won't work on me. Just find something else to do.

Bunny: Alright, if it's not true, then prove me wrong and have a drink with me tonight. I promise I won't bring it up again.

Vijay: Really? You won't talk about this again?

Bunny: Yeah, I promise.

(Of course, we all know promises like these never last for long.)

Vijay: (reluctantly) "Fine. One drink. That's it."

Bunny: (grinning) "Oh, trust me. One drink is all we'll need."

After finishing work, Bunny and Vijay headed back to their room. Determined to prove his point, Bunny bought some liquor, and they made their way to the rooftop of the building. As they poured themselves glasses of whiskey, a moment of silence hung in the air.

Suddenly, breaking the silence, Vijay blurted out, "You know, I know, and I don't even know how to explain it... but I'm just not happy with her."

Bunny: "Oh, really? Tell me something I don't know!"

Vijay: (smiling faintly) "You're an ass, you know that?"

Bunny: "And you're finally admitting what we've all known for months. Progress!"

Vijay, feeling a mixture of relief and embarrassment, looked at Bunny with a mix of surprise and amusement.

Vijay: You always find a way to make me laugh, bro.

Bunny: That's what friends are for, my dear Vijay! Now, let's toast to a night of forgetting all our worries and having a great time together!

With their glasses raised, Bunny and Vijay embraced the comedic relief that came with their rooftop drinking session, ready to momentarily escape their responsibilities and enjoy the lighter side of life.

Bunny saw an opportunity to break Vijay out of his usual routine and bring some excitement into his life. With mischievous intent, Bunny began playing Vijay with more drinks, determined to make this night an unforgettable adventure

Bunny: Cheers, Vijay! Let's make this a night to remember!

Vijay, already feeling the effects of the alcohol, chuckled and raised his glass.

Vijay: To break free from the chains of monotony!

Bunny: That's the spirit! Now, buckle up, my friend. We're going on a wild ride!

As the night wore on and the whiskey flowed, Bunny carefully maneuvered Vijay into agreeing to an impromptu adventure. By the time Vijay realized what was happening, they were cruising through the Bangalore streets, music blaring and Bunny handing him another drink.

Bunny: Vijay, my man! Look at all these city lights. They're dancing just for us!

Vijay, swaying to the music, joined in the fun.

Vijay: You're right, Bunny! This is exactly what I needed. No more boring nights!

Bunny: Absolutely! Tonight, we're the kings of Bangalore!

As the night wore on, Bunny continued to hand Vijay more drinks, fueling his intoxicated state. Vijay, now thoroughly drunk, began to slip into a blissful sleep in the passenger seat.

Bunny, mischievously grinning, whispered to himself.

Bunny: Time for the grand surprise, my snoozing friend.

Hours later, as dawn approached, Vijay began to stir from his slumber. Confused and disoriented, he looked around to find himself standing in front of Goa Airport, alongside Bunny, who had a mischievous grin on his face.

Vijay: "What the hell? Where are we?"

Bunny grinned, slapping him on the back.

Bunny: "Welcome to Goa, buddy! You're free now."

Vijay: Wha... What happened? How did we get here?

Vijay's eyes widened, still struggling to comprehend the situation.

Vijay: But... but how did we end up in Goa? Last I remember, we were in Bangalore!

Bunny, patting Vijay on the back, chuckled.

Vijay: (horrified) "But how?! We were in Bangalore!"

Bunny: My friend, you were having such a great time that you slept through the entire journey! I thought, why not give you the ultimate surprise?

Vijay, a mix of disbelief and awe, couldn't help but laugh at the absurdity of the situation.

Vijay: You sneaky devil, Bunny! I can't believe we actually made it to Goa!

Just as Vijay and Bunny exchanged laughs, they noticed Avi and Shubh approaching them, wearing expressions of both confusion and amusement.

Avi: "Well, look who decided to show up!"

Shubh: (groaning) "I can't believe you maniacs actually pulled this off."

Bunny clapped his hands together, grinning ear to ear.

Bunny: "Gentlemen, the gang is back together. Let's make this a trip to remember—or one we can never talk about again!"

As laughter filled the air, the four friends headed toward their next adventure, ready to trade their frustrations for chaos, fun, and the unpredictable spirit of Goa.

CHAPTER THREE

THE ISLAND OF SECRETS

The gang's arrival in Goa was everything Bunny had promised—sunlit beaches, endless parties, and a promise of chaos. Their first stop was Panjim, the heart of Goa's vibrant nightlife, and Bunny led the charge like a self-proclaimed party general.

Bunny: (raising his arms) "Ladies and gentlemen, welcome to Goa! It's time to unleash the madness. Tonight, we conquer the beaches, tomorrow, the world!"

Avi: (grinning) "Count me in! Let's paint this town in every color available, even the weird ones."

Vijay: (sighing) "Just remember to stay safe. We don't want this trip to turn into a 'Goa Gone Wrong' documentary."

Shubh, feeling a mixture of excitement and anxiety, nodded in agreement.

Shubh: (nervously) "Agreed. Fun is priority one, but let's not end up in the news."

They hopped from beach to beach, blending into the Goan vibe like seasoned partygoers. Chilled beers in hand, they soaked up the sun, laughter, and endless energy of the crowd.

The gang embarked on their journey, hopping from one beach to another, each offering its own unique charm and party scene. They sipped on chilled beers and indulged in cigarettes, immersing themselves in the vibrant Goan atmosphere.

Bunny, with his magnetic personality, seemed to attract adventure wherever he went. On one beach, he spotted a group of lively Russian girls, and without hesitation, he approached them.

Bunny: (striding over) "Excuse me, ladies. Your party seems incomplete without the charm of Bunny. May I join?"

Russian Girl 1: Well, hello there! The more, the merrier! Welcome aboard!

Avi, feeling emboldened by Bunny's audacity, followed suit.

Avi: Mind if I join the party too? Avi's the name, fun's my game!

The group of Russian girls, intrigued by the boys' enthusiasm, welcomed them with open arms. Laughter and banter filled the air as they exchanged stories and shared drinks.

Meanwhile, Vijay and Shubh hung back, enjoying the scene from a quieter corner.

Vijay: (leaning back) "This place is magical. It's like reality took a vacation too."

Shubh: (nodding) "Yeah, but let's hope the magic doesn't come with a price tag."

As evening fell, the gang found themselves at a legendary beach party. Pulsing music, dazzling lights, and euphoric energy surrounded them. Bunny and Avi hit the dance floor, their moves somewhere between enthusiastic and catastrophic.

Bunny: "Avi, tonight we're making history! Or at least a lot of embarrassing memories."

Avi: "Let's do both!"

Vijay and Shubh stayed back, enjoying the lively atmosphere from a safer distance.

Vijay: (smiling) "You know, Shubh, it's moments like these that make the chaos worth it."

Shubh, taking a deep breath and embracing the moment, smiled.

Shubh: That's the beauty of Goa, Vijay. It allows us to find our own balance between wild fun and peaceful moments

As the night progressed, the energy of the party reached a fever pitch. The gang couldn't resist the gravitational pull of chaos and fun, and soon Vijay and Shubh found themselves caught up in the wild whirlwind alongside Bunny and Avi.

Bunny, with his mischievous grin, spotted a limbo stick and wasted no time in organizing an impromptu limbo competition.

Bunny: Ladies and gentlemen, it's time to test your flexibility! Let's see who can limbo the lowest!

Avi, always up for a challenge, eagerly joined in, followed by Vijay and Shubh, who couldn't resist the infectious enthusiasm.

The gang formed a line, bending backward and shimmying under the limbo stick as the crowd cheered them on. Laughter and friendly banter filled the air as they took turns, each trying to outdo the other in a display of sheer determination and hilarious contortions.

Bunny: Vijay, my friend, I never knew you had such hidden limbo skills! You're a limbo superstar!

Vijay, his competitive spirit ignited, grinned and replied.

Vijay: Who would have thought? Limbo could be my hidden talent all along! Let's keep the party going!

With their inhibitions loosened and the adrenaline pumping, the gang let go of their worries and fully embraced the carefree spirit of Goa.

Avi, spotting a group of fire dancers nearby, couldn't resist the opportunity to try his hand at this mesmerizing art form.

Avi: Watch me, guys! I'm about to add some heat to this party!

He bravely approached the fire dancers and, with a combination of awe-inspiring moves and unintentional comedy, joined their mesmerizing performance.

Bunny, Shubh, and Vijay watched in a mix of amazement and amusement as Avi spun, twirled, and dodged the flames with surprising agility.

Bunny: Avi, what the F#! You've set the dance floor on fire, both figuratively and literally!

Avi, slightly singed but undeterred, grinned triumphantly.

Avi: I always knew I had a spark in me, Bunny! Goa brings out the fire in all of us!

As the night progressed, the gang became the life of the party, seamlessly blending into the vibrant tapestry of revelry and creating memories that would last a lifetime.

They danced, they sang, and they laughed until their sides hurt. They jumped from beach to beach, exploring the unique vibes and flavors of each location, leaving their mark everywhere they went.

With their senses heightened and anticipation buzzing, they embarked on a boat journey from Calangute Beach. The wind tousled their hair as they sailed towards an isolated island, shrouded in an air of secrecy and excitement.

Upon reaching the island, their eyes widened as they stumbled upon a party that seemed straight out of a wild fantasy. The beats throbbed through their veins, the smell of smoke filled the air, and drinks flowed like a never-ending river.

Bunny, always the first to dive headlong into adventure, wasted no time in indulging in the potent concoctions that awaited them.

Bunny: This is it, boys! The hub of wildness and pure, unadulterated fun! Let's drink, smoke, and surrender ourselves to the night!

Avi, Vijay, and Shubh, swept up in the intoxicating atmosphere, joined the revelry, their inhibitions melting away like butter in a hot pan. The night blurred into a whirlwind of laughter, music, and the potent haze of substances they dared not fully comprehend.

Morning came with a pounding headache and fragmented memories. Bunny woke up in a dimly lit cabin, his head spinning. As he stumbled around, he discovered Vijay hanging upside down from a ceiling fan, Shubh curled on a bookshelf, and Avi sprawled on a table surrounded by empty bottles.

Bunny woke up groggy, his head pounding as if a marching band was stomping through his skull. He blinked a few times, the blurry outline of the cabin coming into focus.

Bunny: (muttering) "This is it. This is how it ends. Death by... fun?"

As he sat up, he caught sight of something moving outside the cabin door. A large, golden figure sauntered past. Bunny squinted, rubbing his eyes furiously.

Bunny: (yelling) "Guys! GUYS! There's a freaking lion outside! I'm not kidding! A lion! And it looked like it was judging me!"

Avi, sprawled on the floor surrounded by empty bottles, groaned and rolled onto his side.

Avi: (half-asleep) "Bunny, if there's a lion out there, tell it to get in line. My head's already been mauled."

Bunny: "I'm serious, Avi! It had a mane and everything! Either I'm dreaming, or this place is one vodka away from a safari park."

Shubh suddenly sat up, wide-eyed and grinning.

Shubh: (giggling) "A lion? Bro, maybe it's our spirit animal. Like in those motivational posters! 'Unleash the beast!'"

Bunny: (sarcastically) "Yeah, sure, Shubh. Because what this trip really needs is a motivational lion."

Bunny staggered to his feet, stepping over Avi to get a better look at the cabin. That's when he noticed Vijay hanging upside down from the ceiling fan.

Bunny: (yelling) "Oh my God, Vijay's DEAD! He's been sacrificed to the ceiling fan gods!"

Avi bolted upright, clutching his head.

Avi: "Wait, what? Sacrificed?!"

They both rushed to the fan, staring at Vijay's limp body spinning ever so slightly in the air. Blood smeared across his chest added to the horrifying sight.

Avi: (Very Calmly) "Oh no. Oh no. Bunny, do you think he's... shot? Look at the blood! He's definitely shot!"

Bunny: "Why the hell would anyone shoot him and then hang him on a fan?! This isn't a Quentin Tarantino movie!"

Avi grabbed Vijay's arm and shook it desperately.

Avi: "Vijay! Speak to me, man! Are you dead?!"

Vijay stirred groggily, blinking a few times before croaking out a response.

Vijay: "Why am I upside down... and why is Avi crying like someone stole his lunch?"

Relief washed over them, but the absurdity wasn't lost on Bunny.

Bunny: "Dude, you're alive?! And here I was planning your funeral speech. 'He died as he lived—confused and annoyed.'"

Avi and Bunny untangled Vijay from the fan, awkwardly lowering him to the floor.

Avi: "Okay, but why is there blood on your chest?"

Vijay glanced down, his face contorting in confusion.

Vijay: "It's ketchup. I... think I fell into a plate of fries last night?"

Bunny: "Fries! I knew it! You weren't shot, Vijay—you're just a clumsy idiot!"

Meanwhile, Avi tried to stand up, only to slip on an empty bottle and land flat on his back.

Avi: "Seriously, who turned the floor into an ice rink?!"

Bunny, ever the hero, offered a hand but pulled too hard, accidentally sending Avi crashing into the wall.

Avi: (groaning) "You're worse than the floor, Bunny!"

Bunny: "Sorry! My bad. Here, try again. Third time's the charm!"

As Avi finally got to his feet, Shubh was still buzzing with misplaced enthusiasm.

Shubh: "Guys, I've cracked it! We're not hungover—we're chosen! The lion was a sign!"

Bunny: "The only sign we're seeing is 'Danger: Morons Ahead.' Sit down, Shubh, you're giving me a headache."

Shubh, still grinning like a lunatic, declared he needed the restroom. Moments later, a piercing scream tore through the cabin.

Shubh: (screaming) "GUYS! GET IN HERE! NOW!"

The group sprinted to the bathroom, bursting through the door to find Shubh standing frozen, his face pale. Blood was splattered across the walls, and the bathtub was filled with a sickeningly red liquid.

Bunny: (stammering) "What... what the hell is this?! Did we stumble into a crime scene?!"

Avi: (wide-eyed) "This can't be real. It's like a scene out of a horror movie. Where's the creepy soundtrack?!"

Vijay: "We need to get out of here. NOW."

Shubh, his earlier hype drained, pointed shakily at the tub.

Shubh: "The lion... it was warning us. I told you it was a sign!"

Bunny: "Shubh, for the last time, there's no lion! Focus on the murder tub!"

Avi poked his head closer, grimacing at the stench.

Avi: "What is this, tomato soup gone wrong?!"

Vijay leaned closer, noticing something floating in the tub—a blood-soaked bracelet.

Vijay: "It's hers. The girl who brought us here."

The group exchanged terrified glances, the gravity of the situation sinking in.

Their carefree night of partying had taken a horrifying turn. The once-idyllic island now felt like a trap, and their memories, fragmented and hazy, offered no answers.

Bunny: (weakly) "We were just here for fun. How the hell did we end up in a murder mystery?"

Vijay: (shaking his head) "Doesn't matter. We need to figure out what happened, or we won't survive this."

As the group stared at the gruesome scene, the faint sound of rustling came from outside the cabin, sending chills down their spines.

Avi: "Okay, let's all agree—we are never taking Bunny's vacation suggestions again!"

Bunny: (sarcastically) "Oh, sure. Blame me. Because clearly, I planned this blood-soaked mess!"

Shubh: "What if it's the lion? Coming back to finish the job?"

Bunny: "SHUBH, FOR THE LAST TIME—THERE'S. NO. LION!"

The scene ends with the group grabbing whatever they can use as weapons, the tension thick as they brace for whatever horrors await outside the cabin.

CHAPTER FOUR

LET THE STORY BEGIN

The boys gather in the main room of the cabin, each processing the chaos in their unique way. Bunny paces nervously, Avi tries to stay composed, Shubh is visibly uneasy, and Vijay looks irritated but resigned.

Bunny: (throwing his hands up) Alright, guys, someone has to explain this! Who the hell was that girl, and why does this cabin look like a set from a horror movie?

Avi: Bunny. One question at a time. First, who even invited her? Wasn't this supposed to be our trip?

Shubh: Don't look at me! I barely remember anything after that second round of shots.

Vijay: (rolling his eyes) Oh, great. So we've established that nobody knows anything. Fantastic detective work, team!

Bunny: (pointing at Vijay) Don't you start with me! For all we know, it could've been your idea. You've been sneaky ever since you got that new girlfriend.

Vijay: My girlfriend isn't into random islands or blood-splattered bathrooms, thank you very much!

Avi: Maybe she's a long-lost cousin of yours, Bunny. She certainly had your flair for drama.

Bunny: Ha-ha, very funny, Avi. Next time you're drowning in a bathtub full of blood, I'll remember this moment.

Shubh: Let's focus, guys. How did we even get here? The last thing I remember is... (pausing) something about an elephant. Was there an elephant?

Bunny: (throwing a cushion at him) What the hell, Shubh? This isn't Jumanji!

Avi: Or maybe it is. Who knows? Let's just hope we don't have to fight giant mosquitos next.

As the argument about what to do next intensified, Bunny yanked open a cupboard in frustration. His hand emerged holding a ridiculously bright, flamingo-shaped knife.

Bunny: (staring at it) "What the—? Who even makes something like this? A flamingo knife? What were they expecting, a tropical murder spree?"

Vijay: (taking the knife and inspecting it) "Look at this thing. It's pink, cheerful... and horrifyingly sharp. Honestly, this might be the deadliest thing in here."

Avi: (grinning) "Bunny, this knife has your energy written all over it—dangerously annoying but oddly charming."

Shubh: (rolling his eyes) "Yeah, because nothing says 'survivor' like wielding a flamingo-shaped murder weapon."

They burst into laughter, the absurdity of the knife momentarily easing the tension.

Shubh, feeling left out, opened a small drawer on the other side of the room. The moment he pulled it open, a hidden mechanism clicked. Before anyone could react, a wooden beam swung down from above, smacking a dusty plate off the table and sending it crashing to the floor.

Shubh: (stumbling back) "What the—?! Did this cabin come with booby traps?!"

Bunny: "Shubh, buddy, I've said it before, and I'll say it again—you're the worst under pressure."

Avi: (wiping tears of laughter) "At least it wasn't a spear. Knowing this cabin, the next trap will be something completely insane, like flying pineapples."

Shubh glared at them as he rubbed his head, muttering something about bad karma while stepping cautiously away from the drawer.

As they rummaged through the cabin, the group kept uncovering increasingly random and bizarre items.

Avi: (pulling out a can) "Okay, who wants some expired sardines? Best before... oh wow, 2017. Delicious!"

Bunny: "Yeah, nothing screams 'five-star dining' like post-apocalyptic seafood."

Vijay: (lifting a small plastic bag) "Guys, I'm pretty sure this is cocaine."

Shubh: (leaning in) "Wait, is it actually cocaine?"

Vijay: "Either that or it's really weird powdered sugar."

Avi: "Welcome to Goa. Where even the furniture has a drug problem."

Bunny moved to a dusty old chest in the corner, throwing it open with dramatic flair. He froze for a second before bursting into laughter.

Bunny: "Guys, GUESS WHAT I FOUND!"

He held up a handful of faded, poorly lit nude photographs.

Shubh: "Ew! Who even keeps physical copies these days?!"

Avi: (snatching one) "Whoa. Is this... vintage? It's practically an antique! Someone frame it and sell it on eBay!"

Vijay: "We're literally standing in a murder cabin, and you're analyzing photography."

Bunny: (holding up another picture) "Look at this one. The lighting's terrible. Zero stars for composition."

Finally, Vijay, while flipping through couch cushions, pulled out an object with a triumphant grin.

Vijay: "Found it! A phone."

The group crowded around as Vijay held up the device. Its screen was cracked, the edges scuffed, and it looked like it had survived a war.

Avi: "Please tell me it's not another relic like those photos."

Bunny: "Nah, this is Goa. It probably belongs to a drug dealer or a shady politician."

Shubh: "You think it's hers? The girl who brought us here?"

Vijay: "Most likely. Let's see if we can unlock it."

They tried pressing the power button, but the phone wouldn't turn on. Vijay inspected it further, noticing faint bloodstains on the back.

Vijay: "There's blood on it. Looks like it didn't end well for her."

The mood in the cabin shifted as the group exchanged uneasy glances.

Bunny: (trying to lighten the mood) "Or maybe she just had really bad reception and threw it against a wall. Happens to the best of us."

Avi: "Not the time, Bunny!"

As they pondered their next move, the phone vibrated faintly, startling everyone.

Shubh: (jumping back) "It's alive! Oh my God, is this a haunted phone now?!"

Vijay: (frowning) "It turned on!!!"

Avi: (reaching for it) Jackpot! Let's see what's on it.

Bunny: (grinning) Maybe it'll tell us her name or why she dragged us here.

Vijay tries unlocking the phone but fails.

Vijay: Great, it's locked. Typical.

Shubh: (nervously) Can we not open it? What if she comes back and accuses us of snooping?

Bunny: (sarcastically) Oh sure, Shubh. Let's just wait for the blood-soaked girl to politely ask for her phone back. Genius

The boys notice the phone has a fingerprint lock.

Avi: Well, this just got awkward. We need her fingerprint.

Bunny: You mean the girl who's probably either missing or... (gesturing toward the bathroom) worse?

Avi: Unless someone here is a master hacker, I don't see another option.

The group hesitantly made their way to the bathroom, the blood-splattered scene from earlier looking even more grotesque in the harsh daylight. The dried streaks on the walls and the ominous crimson pool in the tub felt almost unreal, like something out of a horror movie set.

As they stood frozen, Avi's sharp eye caught sight of a pale hand peeking out from behind the tub.

Avi: (pointing) "There. Her hand. Let's just... uh... get it over with."

Shubh: (stepping back) "Nope! Nope, nope, nope! This is how every horror movie starts. Someone touches the body, and then BAM! Ghosts!"

Bunny: "Relax, Shubh. We're not summoning demons; we're unlocking a phone. No one's asking you to perform surgery."

Vijay: "Both of you, shut up. We need that phone unlocked."

Vijay, ever the calm one, crouched near the girl's lifeless body. His hand trembled slightly as he reached for hers, careful not to look directly at her face. The eerie silence was broken only by the faint rustle of leaves outside the cabin.

Vijay: "Okay... here goes."

He pressed the girl's thumb against the cracked screen of the phone. The device buzzed faintly, and the lock screen disappeared, revealing a string of cryptic messages from a private number.

Avi: (peeking over Vijay's shoulder) "What does it say?"

Vijay: (reading aloud) "'Meet me at the location. Midnight. Alone.'"

The group exchanged uneasy glances.

Bunny:) "What location? Does it say anything else?"

Vijay: (scrolling) "There's a pinned address. It's somewhere inland. Looks like... a forested area?"

Shubh: "And you want to go there?! Are you insane?!"

Avi: "Insane? Absolutely. But unless you've got a better plan, this is all we've got to go on."

Bunny: (grinning wickedly) "Looks like the adventure just leveled up, boys. We've gone from beach parties to blood-soaked scavenger hunts."

Bunny: (holding up the flamingo knife) "Nobody messes with Bunny and his pink murder bird."

Despite the humor, the unease lingered. Every rustling leaf and distant birdcall felt like a warning.

Avi: (muttering) "This place just keeps getting creepier. If I see one more weird thing, I'm officially done with Goa forever."

As they began to prepare to leave the cabin, a faint buzzing sound caught their attention.

Avi: (freezing) "Uh... guys? The phone just vibrated."

Vijay lifted the phone cautiously, his eyes widening as a new message appeared from the private number.

Vijay: (reading) **"'I'm watching you.'"**

The group froze, their blood running cold. For a moment, no one dared to speak, their breaths shallow and quick.

Shubh:"W-What does that mean? Watching us from where?!"

Vijay: "Okay, no need to panic. It could just be... a really creepy coincidence. Right?"

Avi: (sarcastically) "Oh yeah, because coincidence is totally what this feels like."

The cabin suddenly felt suffocating, every shadow a potential threat. Bunny peeked through the window, scanning the treeline.

Bunny: "I don't see anyone. But... what if they're using drones? Or binoculars? Or... I don't know, creepy jungle voodoo?"

Avi: (sarcastically) "Great, Bunny. Now I'm scared of invisible voodoo spies. Thanks for that."

Bunny: If they are really watching us then there is no point to stay here.

CHAPTER FIVE

WHISPERS IN THE SHADOWS

The four friends reluctantly decided to follow the location on the phone. As they step into the dense forest, an eerie silence descends. Twisted roots and overgrown vines make the trail treacherous, and the occasional animal cry pierces the quiet, unsettling them.

After stumbling out of the cabin, the gang found themselves deep in the dense, claustrophobic jungle. The oppressive heat hung in the air like a thick blanket, making every movement feel sluggish and drenched in sweat. The map they'd found was no help; it seemed to have been drawn by someone who had never seen a real map.

Bunny: (swatting at a branch) "I swear, this jungle is out to get us. It's like the trees are mocking us."

Vijay: (glancing at his phone) "According to this, we should be heading west. But... I don't see a 'west' anywhere. Just more trees and, uh... more trees."

Shubh: "How do you even get lost in a jungle? We're literally surrounded by trees. How hard is it to go... somewhere?"

Avi: (grinning) "Oh, it's easy, Shubh. All you need is a lack of direction and a head full of bad ideas."

They trudged on, trying to follow the trail marked on the hopelessly vague map, when suddenly, Bunny stopped dead in his tracks.

Bunny: "Hold up! What's that noise?"

The group froze. The sound was strange—like something was slithering through the underbrush, and it was getting closer.

Vijay: (whispering) "Maybe it's a snake?"

Bunny: "A snake? In this heat? Are you kidding me? I'll take a bear over a snake."

Avi: "Just don't panic. I've got this!"

Without warning, Avi whipped out a stick and started wildly waving it in the air.

Avi: (yelling) "Come at me, nature! I'll show you who's boss!"

Everyone stared in horror as Avi continued to flail the stick around like a madman. Suddenly, a small, harmless lizard scurried out from behind a bush, causing Avi to jump back with a yelp.

Avi: (frantically) "It's a... it's a...!"

Bunny: (laughing) "Really? You're scared of a lizard?"

Avi: (breathing heavily) "That thing was... evil. Look at those eyes!"

They all burst into laughter, the absurdity of the situation lightening the tension, but the reality of being lost soon sank in again.

Vijay: "We're never going to find this place if we keep going in circles."

Bunny: (hands on his hips) "You're right. I mean, I'm sure 'west' is around here somewhere, but it's like every direction looks the same. Like a bad acid trip."

Suddenly, Shubh, who had been walking a few paces behind them, stumbled and fell face-first into a pile of leaves. The group rushed over to help him, only to discover he had fallen into what looked like a giant puddle of mud.

Shubh: "I hate my life right now."

Bunny: "Not your best landing, buddy."

Avi: (mocking) "Should've taken that left turn at Albuquerque!"

Shubh groaned as he stood up, covered in mud.

Shubh: "If we survive this jungle, I'm never looking at another puddle the same way again."

Vijay: "Okay, that's it. We're using the stars. No more maps, no more directions. The sky doesn't lie."

Shubh: "But genius, its still day where will you find the Stars?"

As they looked up to the sky, trying to make sense of the stars above, a screeching noise erupted from nearby bushes, causing them to jump back in unison.

Bunny: (eyes wide) "What the hell is that?!"

The group slowly turned their heads toward the noise. After a long, tense pause, a tiny monkey popped out from the bush, holding a half-eaten banana in its hands.

Avi: (relieved) "It's just a monkey, guys. You scared of that, too?"

Shubh: (wiping mud off his face) "At this point, I'd be more terrified if it wasn't a monkey. What's next? A lion in a tutu?"

Bunny: (laughing) "What the hell now a Monkey. Shubh it is Jumanji am taking my words back. You know what? Let's just keep following this monkey. At least it knows where the party is."

They all chuckled at the idea, following the mischievous creature as it bounded off through the jungle. The absurdity of the situation lifted their spirits, but they still hadn't found the right path—or the answers they were seeking.

Bunny: (looking around nervously) So... when does this forest turn into Narnia? Because right now, it's giving Blair Witch vibes.

Vijay: Bunny, can you just be serious for once? We're trying to figure out why our lives are spiraling into a horror movie!

Bunny:Relax, Mr. Responsible. Maybe this is all just a bad prank. Someone's probably filming us right now for a reality show. Smile for the hidden cameras!

Avi: Both of you, shut up. We need to focus.

Shubh: Focus on what? Getting murdered by the tree people? I told you this was a bad idea!

As they move deeper, the path leads to a cluster of old houses. The locals there seem unfriendly—watching them silently, their expressions hard and unwelcoming.

Vijay: Don't look them in the eye. Just keep walking.

One old woman mutters something in a language none of them understand. A man steps out of a hut, holding a machete, and glares at them.

Bunny: (whispering) So... friendly neighborhood vibes, huh? Maybe we should ask them for directions.

Shubh: (hissing) Are you insane? That guy looks like he chops tourists for breakfast!

As they hurry past the village, the forest thickens, and they come across a decrepit church with broken stained-glass windows. The air inside feels heavy and suffocating. Avi lingers for a moment, staring at the graffiti on the wall—a strange symbol that seems to unsettle him.

Vijay: (noticing Avi) Hey, what's with you? Why do you keep acting like you know something?

Avi: I don't. Let's just keep moving.

Bunny: Oh, come on. You've been acting weird this whole time. First the cabin, now this creepy church—how the hell do you know so much about this place?

Avi: I said I don't know anything! Let's go!

As they continue, the sound of an engine cuts through the forest. A car speeds toward them on the narrow dirt path.

Shubh: Holy shit! She's going to ram us!

The boys scatter as the car screeches to a halt. A young woman steps out, her face flushed with urgency.

Girl: (angrily) Are you trying to get yourselves killed? What the hell are you doing here?

Vijay: We could ask you the same thing.

Girl: (ignoring him) Sit in the car. Now.

The boys hesitate, but the girl's tone is commanding.

Shubh: What if she's worse than the machete guy?

Bunny: Oh, great idea, Shubh. Let's walk back to Murder Village.

Reluctantly, they climb into the car. As they drive, the girl glares at them through the rearview mirror.

Girl: Start talking. Who are you, and why the hell do you have her phone?

Avi: Her? Who are you talking about?

Girl: Don't play dumb. I've been tracking this phone. Where did you find it, and why are you heading to that location?

Vijay: Look, we don't know what's going on either. We woke up in a cabin with her phone and no memory of how we got there.

Bunny: If you're tracking her, maybe you can tell us what's going on!

The girl's face tightens, and she grips the steering wheel harder.

Girl: I was hoping you could answer that.

As the tension rises, Avi suddenly speaks.

Avi: Wait... I think I remember something.

Everyone turns to him, the air in the car growing heavy with anticipation.

Avi: (pausing) Last night... There was a boat. And someone is screaming.

Vijay: A boat? I don't remember that at all.

Shubh:What are you talking about, Avi? None of us were near a boat!

Avi: I'm not making this up! There was a dock, and... (pausing) someone was chasing us.

The group falls silent, confusion and paranoia spreading among them.

Bunny: Are you sure you're not just making this up, Avi?

Avi: (angrily) Why would I lie about something like this?

Before the argument escalates, a deafening explosion shakes the car. The girl slams on the brakes as smoke rises from a nearby clearing.

Their phones buzz simultaneously. A message flashes on the screen:

"This time, you're lucky. Next time, you won't be."

The girl looks at them, her face pale.

Girl: (whispering) What the hell did you idiots get yourselves into?

In the distance, a shadowy figure emerges from the smoke, watching them.

Vijay: Is... is that someone standing there?

The figure steps closer, but before they can see clearly, the girl slams the gas, speeding away.

Bunny: (yelling) What was that? Who was that?!

Girl: If we're lucky, we won't have to find out.

The car speeding away, tension thick in the air, and the shadowy figure disappearing into the trees.

CHAPTER SIX

INTO THE HIDEOUT

The car sped through the uneven jungle trail, the headlights cutting through the darkness. The tension inside the car was palpable. Vijay sat in the passenger seat, quietly observing the girl who had inexplicably saved them. In the backseat, Bunny, Avi, and Shubh huddled together, whispering furiously.

Bunny: (leaning close to Avi and Shubh) "Guys, are we seriously just going to trust her? She popped out of nowhere, said, 'Come with me if you want to live,' and now we're following her like this is Madgaon Express!?"

Avi: "To be fair, that's more dangerous than lost in the jungle."

Shubh: (whispering) "Bunny has a point. She could be leading us straight into a trap. For all we know, this could turn into Go Goa Gone any minute. Next thing you know, she'll tell us the gang we pissed off is zombies."

Bunny: (mock horror) "Or worse—imagine she's one of them! She takes us to the hideout, and bam! We're tied up like chickens ready for slaughter."

They all snickered, but the laughter died quickly as they exchanged uneasy glances.

Shubh: (glancing nervously at the girl) "I still don't get why she saved us. What if she's working with the gang? Maybe she's their bait to make us trust her."

Bunny: "Yeah, because nothing screams 'trustworthy' like showing up in a jungle that explodes five minutes later. What was that, her dramatic entrance?"

Avi: (nodding) "Classic Dil Chahta Hai—except instead of friends heading to Goa for fun, it's us heading to... I don't even know where. Our doom?"

Bunny: "At least in Dil Chahta Hai, they had beaches and safe roads. We have mud, potholes, and a driver we met 20 minutes ago!"

Vijay turned around from the front seat, his voice a sharp whisper.

Vijay: "Can you idiots keep it down? She can hear you!"

Bunny: (hissing back) "Good! Maybe she'll tell us why she's acting like Goa's answer to James Bond!"

Shubh: "Seriously, Vijay, do you even trust her? She hasn't told us her name, her plan, or why she's helping us. What if she's leading us to a gang den and we're the main course?"

The girl glanced briefly in the rearview mirror, smirking as if she had overheard every word.

Girl: "If I wanted to kill you, I'd have left you in the jungle. That explosion wasn't for decoration, you know."

The gang froze, caught red-handed.

Avi: (forcing a smile) "No one's questioning your heroism, ma'am. We're just, uh... brainstorming our next steps."

Bunny: "Yeah, like whether we'll die in one piece or get chopped up into kebabs."

The car hit a bump, jolting everyone. Bunny took the opportunity to lean toward Avi and Shubh.

Bunny: "Okay, hear me out. What if she's taking us hostage? She'll call the gang and demand a ransom."

Avi: (raising an eyebrow) "Ransom from whom? Have you seen our bank accounts? The only thing they'd get from us is IOUs and leftover Maggi packets."

Shubh: "Or she could kill us and sell our organs on the black market. I heard kidneys fetch a decent price these days."

Bunny: (clutching his stomach) "Not my kidneys! I need those for... you know... living!"

Avi: "Relax, Bunny. With your alcohol consumption, your kidneys are probably worthless. She'd make more selling your liver as a coaster."

The group burst into muffled laughter, drawing another sharp glance from Vijay.

Vijay: (turning to the girl, cautiously) "So, where exactly are you taking us?"

The girl didn't answer immediately, her hands gripping the steering wheel tightly as she navigated the bumpy road.

Girl: "Somewhere safe. Or as safe as you can be after pissing off the biggest gang in Goa."

Bunny: (to Avi and Shubh) "See? She's not even denying it. This is how it starts in every Bollywood thriller. First, they 'help' you. Then, they double-cross you. Next thing you know, we're tied to chairs, reenacting Go Goa Gone!"

Avi: "If she's Saif Ali Khan in this scenario, does that make you Kunal Khemu?"

Bunny: "Only if you're the first to die, Avi."

Shubh: "Guys, focus. We don't even know if we're the heroes of this story. For all we know, we're the clueless sidekicks who get picked off first."

Bunny: (leaning forward dramatically) "I refuse to die in this jungle! If anyone's going to double-cross us, they better do it somewhere with Wi-Fi!"

The girl sighed audibly, her patience clearly wearing thin.

Girl: "If you don't shut up, I'll stop this car right now and leave you here for the gang to find."

The threat silenced them momentarily, but not without a few exchanged smirks.

The girl drives them to a remote location—a dilapidated bungalow overrun with vines and surrounded by dense jungle. The atmosphere is heavy with unease, and the boys exchange nervous glances.

Bunny: So... are we staying at a haunted Airbnb now?

Vijay: Bunny, can you for once just keep quiet?

Avi: (sarcastically) Let's not forget we're in the middle of nowhere with someone who hasn't even told us her name. Great job trusting her, Vijay.

Girl: My name is Maya. And if you keep talking, I'll leave you here for the gang to find.

The boys fall silent as Maya leads them inside. The hideout is sparse but eerie: newspapers with bold headlines like "Gang Wars Ravage Goa" are pinned to the walls. A shelf holds knives and a gun. One corner is stained with blood, but it's unclear if it's old or new.

Maya pulls out a map and places it on a table, marking the pinned location they were headed to.

Maya: That's where my sister was last seen alive. The same night you four morons decided to waltz into a gangster's party.

Shubh: Wait, what? We were at their party?

Maya: You don't remember? How convenient.

Vijay: We don't remember. If we did, don't you think we'd have gotten the hell out of here by now?

Maya: Or maybe you're lying. Maybe one of you was working with them.

The accusation sends the group into chaos.

Avi: (to Vijay) Oh, perfect! Another reason to doubt you, Mr. Leader. How do you always know where to go and what to do, huh?

Vijay: (angrily) Shut up, Avi. You have no idea what you're talking about.

Bunny: Guys, let's not fight. Maybe Maya's just bluffing to freak us out, right? (turning to Maya) Right?

Maya doesn't respond, leaving the group in growing paranoia.

As the gang tries to break into the hideout, Maya frantically directs the boys to help set traps or arm themselves. The tension is thick, but Bunny can't help being himself.

Bunny: (holding up a frying pan) What am I supposed to do with this? Cook them breakfast?

Maya: (gritting her teeth) Hit them in the head if they get in! Aim for the soft spot!

Bunny: (mocking) Oh, sure. Because I'm an expert on gangster anatomy.

Suddenly, the front door bursts open, and the first gangster charges in. Bunny swings the frying pan wildly and lands a hit... squarely on Vijay's arm.

Vijay: (yelling) That's my soft spot, you idiot!

Bunny: Sorry! Reflexes!

Maya lunges forward, disarming the gangster with brutal precision and stabbing him in the leg. Blood sprays onto Shubh's shirt, and he screams.

Shubh: (freaking out) Oh my God, this is a designer! I'm going to die unfashionable!

Maya: (grabbing Shubh by the collar) Shut up or you'll die, period!

As more gangsters rush in, Bunny backs into a cabinet and accidentally pulls a string that triggers a hidden mechanism. Knives shoot out from the wall, impaling a gangster mid-scream. His body slumps against the wall, pinning another gangster beneath him.

Bunny: Holy shit! That actually worked?!

Maya: (deadpan) Congratulations. You're a murderer.

Bunny: I—I'm a hero! There's a difference, right?

Meanwhile, Shubh tries to sneak toward the back door but slips on a pool of blood. He lands face-first, his mouth brushing against a severed finger.

Shubh: (spitting and gagging) OH GOD! WHAT IS THIS?! AM I A CANNIBAL NOW?!

As Shubh scrambles to his feet, he accidentally kicks the severed finger at another gangster, hitting him square in the eye. The gangster howls, clutching his face.

Avi: Did you just blind someone with a finger?

Shubh: I DON'T KNOW! I WANT TO GO HOME!

A gangster charges at Avi, wielding a machete. Avi grabs a nearby lamp and smashes it over the gangster's head. The bulb explodes in a shower of sparks, setting the gangster's hair on fire.

Gangster: (screaming and flailing) "mhaka vachaya! mhaka vachaya" ("Save me! Save me!")

Avi: Dude, stop, drop, and roll! It's basic survival!

The flaming gangster stumbles into the curtains, setting them ablaze. Smoke starts filling the room as chaos erupts.

Maya grabs a broken bottle and slashes another gangster's face, blood spraying across the room. She turns to the boys, her face splattered with gore, and yells:

Maya: If you don't fight, you're next!

The boys scramble to arm themselves with whatever they can find:

Bunny picks up a stapler and manages to shoot staples into a gangster's hand, causing him to scream in pain.

Vijay grabs a table leg and clubs a gangster over the head, sending teeth flying.

Shubh, still panicking, hurls a random potted plant, hitting a gangster in the groin.

Gangster: (collapsing in agony) "hache khatira tumi pharika karatale" ("You'll pay for this!")

As the fight rages, Bunny triggers another trap—a weighted net falls from the ceiling, catching two gangsters and crushing one beneath its weight.

Bunny: (laughing nervously) Hey, I think I'm getting the hang of this!

Suddenly, one of the gangsters pulls a gun and fires, narrowly missing Vijay. The boys scream and rush toward the back door. Maya shoots the gangster in the leg, then grabs Bunny by the collar.

Maya: Move your ass, or I'll feed you to them myself!

They burst through the back door into the jungle, leaving behind a scene of blood and destruction.

As they run, Vijay stumbles and falls. He clutches his head as fragmented memories flood back:

A girl's scream.

Bunny shouting, "Get off her!"

Vijay throwing a punch, his fist colliding with someone's jaw.

Blood dripped from his knuckles.

Vijay: (whispering) "It was... it was me. I was there."

The others stop, turning to look at him.

Bunny: Vijay, what are you talking about?

Before Vijay can explain, a loud explosion rocks the jungle. Flames erupt in the distance, and the gang leader's voice echoes through the trees:

Gang Leader: "mhaka para kellyana tuka pashchatapa jatalo!" ("You'll regret crossing me!")

Maya's phone buzzes with a message:

"You got away this time. Next time, you won't be so lucky."

The group stares at each other, bloodied and terrified, as they realize the nightmare is far from over.

CHAPTER SEVEN

FEAR FACTOR

The group stumbles through the dense forest, their breaths ragged. The explosion still echoes in the distance, and flickers of flames illuminate the darkened sky. Maya leads the way, her face set in a grim expression, while the boys lag behind, shaken and bloodied.

Bunny: Okay, is it just me, or do we officially suck at this whole 'staying alive' thing?

Shubh: I think I swallowed blood. Is that bad? Am I going to turn into one of them?

Avi: What do you mean, them? They're gangsters, not zombies, you idiot!

Vijay: Will all of you just shut up?! We're not safe yet!

Maya suddenly halts and gestures for silence. The group freezes as faint voices drift through the trees. The gang is still hunting them.

Maya: We need to move faster. They won't stop until we're dead.

Avi: "Can someone please tell me who the hell these lunatics are? They're trying to kill us, and we don't even know why! What kind of horror show are we starring in?"

Vijay: "Yeah, exactly! Did we stumble into some twisted reality TV where the prize is a slow, painful death? Because

I'm ready to walk off set now."

Maya: (leaning in with a sly, unsettling smirk) "Alright, you want answers? Buckle up, boys. These psychos chasing you are part of The Shadows—Goa's very own nightmare fuel. They're not just any gang; they're the kind that runs the 'we ruin lives for fun' business: drugs, trafficking, extortion...you name it. And guess what? Their motto is simple—'If you're a problem, you're a corpse.'"

Avi: (gulping) "That's...comforting."

Maya: "Oh, I'm just getting started. The gang has two top dogs—the leader, who's basically Goa's version of the Grim Reaper, and his younger brother, a sociopath with a smile that could freeze hell. They don't just kill you—they make it a performance piece. And last night, thanks to your little heroic outburst, you've earned a starring role in their next horror flick."

Vijay: "Wait. Hold on. What exactly did we do to tick them off? I mean, Bunny threw a few punches, but surely that's not worth a death sentence, right?"

Maya: (raising an eyebrow) "Oh, sweet summer child. You didn't just tick them off. You danced on their nerves in flaming tap shoes. Congratulations, boys. You're now public enemy number one in Goa. Consider it a promotion...to hell."

(A faint echo of laughter drifts through the Forest, distant yet chilling, as if the gang is already enjoying their prey's terror. A gust of wind rattles the boys, and the boys felt the fear from top to down and every part if their body, amplifying the unsettling vibe.)

Avi: "Please tell me they're just regular killers and not, like, ghost gangsters or something. I swear I'll die faster from anxiety than whatever they've planned."

Maya: "Oh, they're very real. And very human. But trust me, they'll make you wish they were ghosts by the time they're done."

Bunny: Wow, love the pep talk. Super motivational.

As they push forward, Vijay begins to feel lightheaded. He clutches his head, fragmented memories of the previous night surfacing.

Flashback:"*A crowded party with loud music. Bunny is yelling at someone while Vijay stands in front of a girl, shielding her.*

A knife glinting in the moonlight. Vijay grabbing someone's arm and twisting it until they scream.

The girl sobbing, saying, "Thank you," before leading them away."

Vijay stumbles, and Maya turns to steady him.

Maya: What's wrong with you?

Vijay: I... I was there. At the party. I saw her—your sister.

The others stop in their tracks, staring at him.

Bunny: What are you saying, Vijay? You remember?

Avi: And you're just telling us now? What else are you hiding?

Shubh: Oh my God, we're going to die because of Vijay! I knew he was bad luck!

Maya: (grabbing Vijay's arm) What else do you remember? Tell me!

Vijay: (shaking his head) I don't know... It's blurry. There was a fight. She was scared. I... I tried to protect her.

Maya's grip tightens, her expression unreadable.

Maya: You'd better hope you're telling the truth.

As they continue, they stumble upon a clearing where the gang had been camping. The remnants of their presence are scattered: bloodied rags, a half-empty bottle of whiskey, and a rusted machete.

Shubh: (looking at the machete) Okay, that's not creepy at all. Totally normal forest picnic vibes.

Bunny: Maybe they were just lumberjacks... really angry, homicidal lumberjacks.

Maya: Focus. Look for anything useful.

Bunny: I am missing the Flamingo Knife right now...
Avi: Then why did you left it there?

As the group searches the abandoned campsite, the unease in the air is palpable. Shubh stumbles and lets out a sharp scream, landing face-first into the dirt.

Shubh: Ugh, what the hell did I trip on this time?

He rolls over, brushing dirt off his face, when his hand touches something cold and rubbery. He glances down and recoils in horror—it's a severed arm, the flesh gray and decayed.

Shubh: OH MY GOD! OH MY GOD! WHAT IS THAT?!

The others rush to him, and Maya immediately kneels down, her expression dark. She begins digging with her hands, uncovering more of the decomposed body beneath.

Shubh: Nope. Nope, nope, nope. I did not sign up for this.

Avi: What the hell is this? Some kind of sick message?

As Maya digs deeper, they uncover the corpse's face—bloated and disfigured, with one eye partially eaten away by insects. Blood has long since dried around the gaping wound on his throat. His fingers are curled into claws, as if he died struggling.

Shubh: I'm gonna puke. Someone stop me. I'm gonna puke!

Maya: There's something in his hand.

Maya pries open the corpse's stiff fingers with a sickening crack. Clutched in the hand is a crumpled photograph, smudged with dried blood. She unfolds it carefully, revealing a group of gangsters posing near a car, all grinning menacingly.

On the back of the photo, the words "Finish what we started" are scrawled in shaky writing.

Avi: What... what the hell does that mean?

Maya: It means they weren't just after you. They were after all of us.

As Maya inspects the grave, Bunny begins to look around nervously.

Bunny: (muttering) Why is it so quiet? Where are the birds? There should be birds, right?

Shubh: Oh my God, Bunny, stop talking about birds and start worrying about dead people!

Avi freezes as he notices something nearby—a trail of blood leading to a second, smaller grave. The dirt here is fresher, the mound still damp. He backs away, pointing shakily.

Avi: Uh, Maya? I think there's... there's another one.

Maya follows his gaze and curses under her breath.

Maya: Start digging.

Shubh: Are you insane?! I am not digging up another corpse!

Maya: Fine. Sit there and wait for the gang to catch up. They'll be happy to add you to the collection.

Maya begins digging furiously. Bunny joins her hesitantly, his hands trembling as he moves the dirt. As they dig, the rancid stench of decay grows stronger. Flies buzz around them, landing on their faces and arms.

Finally, they uncover a burlap sack, its edges soaked with blood. Maya carefully slices it open with her knife, and the contents spill out:

A severed head, its face frozen in terror.

Pieces of jewelry—a bracelet, a necklace, and an anklet—gleaming through the gore.

A stack of Polaroid photos, each showing someone tied up and gagged, fear etched into their features.

Shubh: OH MY GOD! WHAT IS THIS? WHAT THE HELL IS THIS?!

Vijay: That... that bracelet. Didn't the girl at the party have one just like it?

The group exchanges horrified looks as the realization sinks in.

Avi: This can't be real. This can't be happening.

Maya: (grimly, holding up the photos) It's real. And it's going to get worse.

The gruesome finds push the group closer to their breaking point:

Shubh starts hyperventilating, muttering about how they're all going to die.

Avi refuses to move, his hands shaking as he repeats, "This isn't real. This isn't real."

Bunny tries to take charge, yelling at everyone to pull themselves together, but his voice wavers.

Vijay becomes eerily quiet, staring at the severed head as flashes of the girl at the party flood his mind.

Vijay: She... she was wearing that bracelet. I remember now.

Maya grabs him by the shoulders, shaking him.

Maya: (desperately) What else do you remember? Tell me!

Vijay: (stammering) There was... a fight. I hit someone. Blood everywhere. She was screaming... I—I think I...

He trails off, unable to finish. Maya lets go, her face unreadable, and stands abruptly.

Maya: We can't stay here. Move. Now.

As they leave the gravesite, the group steps through more signs of carnage—a tree marked with bloody handprints, shredded clothes hanging from branches, and a trail of entrails leading deeper into the forest.

Bunny: This isn't a forest. It's a goddamn slaughterhouse.

The group doesn't respond, their silence heavy with fear.

Before they leave, Maya notices something carved into the tree near the gravesite:

"vishvasaghataka ragata vhamvapaka jaya" ("Betrayal must bleed.")

She traces the letters with her fingers, her jaw tightening.

Maya: (to herself) They think it's revenge. But they don't know the truth.

Avi: (overhearing) What truth?

Maya doesn't answer, leading them deeper into the forest as the gang's voices grow louder behind them.

CHAPTER EIGHT

THE ENCOUNTER

The jungle felt alive, pulsing with sounds that made the group's skin crawl. Crickets chirped incessantly, their sharp cries cutting through the heavy air. Somewhere nearby, an owl hooted, its haunting call echoing like a warning. The thick canopy above blocked out most of the moonlight, leaving the path ahead shrouded in eerie shadows.

Shubh: I swear, the trees are closing in on us.

Bunny: Relax, Shubh. It's not the trees you need to worry about—it's the snakes.

Shubh froze mid-step, staring at a rustling bush.

Maya: Keep moving! If the gang doesn't get us, the leopards will.

The scent of damp earth and decaying leaves filled their noses, mingling with the saltiness of sweat and fear. Each step seemed to unleash unseen creatures—a startled lizard scuttled across Avi's foot, and Shubh yelped as something brushed against his arm.

Avi: This is why people stick to beaches and margaritas.

In the distance, the faint sound of waves crashing reminded them they were still near the coast. But the jungle, dense and unyielding, felt like an entirely different world—wild, untamed, and deadly.

The group sprints through the jungle, the gang's shouts echoing behind them. Branches slap their faces, roots trip their feet, and the air grows heavy with tension.

Maya: Keep moving! They're closing in!

Bunny: Yeah, I know! I can hear them! What's your next genius plan? Run until we turn into skeletons?

Shubh: Bunny, shut up! I can't deal with your jokes right now!

Suddenly, a gunshot rings out, the bullet grazing a tree inches from Shubh's head. He yelps and ducks instinctively.

Shubh: THEY'RE SHOOTING AT US! THIS ISN'T A MOVIE, GUYS!

Vijay: (grabbing Shubh) Get up, or you're as good as dead!

Maya spots a steep incline leading to a narrow ravine below. She stops and points.

Maya: Down there. It'll give us cover.

Avi: (staring at the drop) Are you insane? We'll break our legs!

Maya: Better broken legs than bullet holes. Move!

One by one, they slide down the incline, dirt and rocks tumbling with them. Bunny loses his balance midway and crashes into Avi, sending them both tumbling into a shallow stream at the bottom.

Bunny: See? Broken everything. Great plan.

Maya: (helping him up) Shut up and keep moving.

As they regroup in the ravine, Vijay stumbles, clutching his head as more memories flood back:

Flashback: The girl at the party crying, "They'll kill me if I don't go with them."
Bunny shouting, "Over my dead body!" and lunging at a gangster.

Vijay punches someone, his hands dripping with blood. The girl leading them out of the party.

Vijay collapses to his knees, gasping.

Maya: What's wrong with you now?

Vijay: I remember. The party... your sister...

Everyone freezes, their eyes fixed on him.

Bunny: (wide-eyed) You do? What happened?

Vijay: (struggling to speak) She was scared. They... they tried to take her. We fought them. But then...

Maya: But what? What happened to her?

Before Vijay can answer, another gunshot rings out. The group scatters, ducking behind rocks as bullets rain down into the ravine.

The group scrambles for cover behind large rocks. The gunshots echo, and the gang's shouts grow louder. Maya peers over the rock, her face tense.

Maya: They're driving us toward the ravine. If they corner us there, we're done for.

Bunny: (frustrated) Oh great, so it's another day of "How Do We Die Horribly?" What's the plan?

Maya: I don't know! Just stay quiet!

Vijay scans the area, his jaw tightening as he spots a cluster of precariously balanced boulders perched above a narrow choke point. The gang will have to pass directly beneath them.

Vijay: (pointing) Bunny, look. Those boulders.

Bunny: (blinking) Yeah, big rocks. Super useful. Can we eat them? Or maybe hurl them one at a time and hope for the best?

Vijay: No, idiot. We can drop them—all of them.

Bunny: Ohhhh. You mean... murder by landslide?

Maya: That's insane. It'll take too long—

Vijay: (cutting her off) It's our best shot. Bunny, you with me?

Bunny: You're asking if I want to risk my life to chuck rocks at homicidal maniacs? Hell yeah, I'm in.

Bunny and Vijay climb toward the boulders, slipping on loose dirt as they work their way up the incline. Below, Maya and the others keep watch, their breathing shallow.

Shubh: (whispering to Maya) Are they actually doing this? This feels like a terrible idea.

Maya: Do you have a better one?

Shubh: Yeah, run until we die of old age!

At the top, Bunny and Vijay start wedging rocks loose, their fingers scraped and bloody. One boulder shifts suddenly, nearly crushing Bunny.

Bunny: Okay, that was close! I like my limbs attached, thanks!

Vijay: Less whining, more pushing!

Finally, the boulders teeter precariously. The gang approaches the choke point below, unaware of the trap.

Vijay: (to Bunny) On three. One... two...

Before Vijay can say three, Bunny kicks the nearest boulder.

Bunny: (shouting) Surprise, assholes!

The boulder tumbles, colliding with the others and creating a massive landslide. The rocks crash down with thunderous force, crushing two gangsters instantly. One gangster is thrown against the ravine wall, his body twisted at an unnatural angle. Blood sprays across the ground as the others scatter, yelling in Konkani.

Gang Member 1: "kaya naraka mhanalyara phatim saruna svataka vachavapa!" ("What the hell is that back off and save yourself!")

Bunny and Vijay scramble back down, their faces pale but triumphant.

Bunny: Boom. Rockslide of death. You're welcome.

Shubh: Oh my God. There's... there's so much blood. I think I'm going to pass out.

Maya: (looking at Vijay) That was reckless. But... It worked.

Vijay: (staring at the bodies) We didn't have a choice.

Bunny: Yeah, uh, choice or no choice, let's not make "crushing people with rocks" a habit, okay?

As the group regains their composure, they hear the gang regrouping in the distance.

Maya: Don't just stand there! They'll be back any second. Move!

They flee deeper into the jungle, leaving behind the gruesome scene of crushed bodies and smeared blood.

The group pauses briefly after fleeing the site of the landslide. The gang's pursuit has temporarily slowed, but their shouts echo faintly through the trees. Avi helps Shubh steady himself, who is still shaking from the bloodbath they left behind.

Shubh: (muttering) I can't believe we just did that. We killed people. Killed them.

Bunny: Relax, Shubh. Think of it as... aggressive self-defense. Really aggressive.

Shubh: Oh, sure! Let me just update my resume: "Excellent at mass murder with a side of trauma!"

Maya: (cutting them off) Quiet! They're regrouping. We need to keep moving.

As they press on, the jungle begins to thin, revealing a large clearing ahead. The group stops abruptly, their breath catching as they take in the sight before them.

The clearing is dominated by a small wooden shack, dilapidated and leaning to one side. In front of it stands the gang leader—a tall, imposing man with a scar down his face, flanked by two heavily armed gangsters.

Gang Leader: (calmly, in Konkani) "kityaka bhandana dhamvapacho italo yatna karatata. tumi sagale aja ratim marapache asata." ("Why the fuck are you trying so hard to run. You all are going to die tonight.")

The gang leader steps forward, his boots crunching on the gravel, and looks at the group with a predatory grin.

Gang Leader: (mocking) Look at you. Just a bunch of scared little rats. Did you think you'd come to Goa and leave without paying the price? Do you know where you are? This isn't some Instagram beach. This is my Goa. My family built this underworld from the sand up. These streets? These beaches? They're ours. Even the cops don't piss without asking my permission.

He smirked, taking a step closer.

Gang Leader: (switching to Konkani) "hangasara sagale amakam kityaka bhiyetata hachi yada karuna ditam." ("I'll remind you why everyone here fears us.")

The group exchanged uneasy glances, the weight of his words settling in.

Vijay steps forward, his fists clenched.

Vijay: Whatever you want, take it out on me. Leave them out of this.

The gang leader laughs, a harsh, guttural sound that echoes in the clearing.

Gang Leader: (shaking his head) Oh, it's not that simple, hero. You see, it's not just about you. (gestures to the group) It's about all of you stepping into my world, my territory, and thinking you could walk away unscathed.

He circles them, his voice growing darker.

Gang Leader: You embarrassed me. At that party. In front of my men. My brother. Do you have any idea what that means? If word gets out that I let you live after what you did... (pauses, leans in) I lose everything.

Maya narrows her eyes, her voice sharp despite her fear.

Maya: All this... for your ego?

The gang leader whirls on her, his expression hardening.

Gang Leader: Ego? No, little girl. It's about power. Power is what keeps these streets in line, keeps my men loyal, and keeps people like you afraid.

He points at Vijay, his voice rising.

Gang Leader: And you? You stabbed my brother. You think I'm just going to let that go? He was blood. Blood demands blood.

The group is silent, the weight of his words sinking in.

Gang Leader: So here's how it goes: give me him, and the rest of you walk away. Refuse... (his smile widens) and I'll make sure your screams are the last sound this jungle hears.

Maya: You. You're the one who killed my sister.

The gang leader tilts his head, his scarred face lit by the dim moonlight.

Gang Leader: Ah, the grieving sibling. Such devotion. It's almost touching. But tell me, Maya, did your sister ever tell you how deep in shit she was?

Maya stiffens, her fists clenching.

Maya: Don't you dare talk about her.

The gang leader ignores her, turning his gaze to Vijay.

The leader's smirk widens as he points at Vijay.

Vijay's jaw tightens, flashes of the fight at the party flickering in his mind. He doesn't respond, but the leader's words hit like a hammer.

Gang Leader: (laughing) Oh, he didn't tell you? Brave little Vijay here stabbed one of my men. (leaning in) And not just any man. My brother.

The revelation shocks the group. Maya's eyes widen as she steps back, staring at Vijay.

Avi: Vijay... is that true?

Vijay: It was self-defense. He was trying to take her!

Gang Leader: Ah, the righteous hero act. How noble. But heroes die just like everyone else. And tonight, you'll pay for what you did.

The gang leader pulls out a phone and types a message. A moment later, Maya's phone buzzes. She hesitates before reading the text aloud:

Maya: (reading) "Bring him to me, or I'll kill them all."

The group looks at each other, panic setting in.

Shubh: What does that mean?

The gang leader points at Vijay.

Gang Leader: Him. The murderer. Hand him over, and I'll let the rest of you go.

Bunny: Like hell we will!

Gang Leader: Then I'll take all of you. Your choice.

The group is paralyzed, caught between betrayal and survival. Vijay steps forward, his fists clenched.

Vijay: (to Maya) Don't listen to him. He's lying.

Gang Leader: (smiling) Am I? Or are you just too scared to admit the truth?

Before Maya can respond, a sharp sound cuts through the clearing—a single gunshot. The group ducks instinctively as the gang leader lowers his smoking gun.

Gang Leader: Tick tock, little rats. You don't have forever.

The gang leader and his men step back toward the shack, leaving the group frozen in fear as they realize their time is running out.

CHAPTER NINE

THE BREAKING POINT

The gang leader and his men retreat into the shack, leaving the group stunned in the jungle clearing. Maya grips her phone tightly, rereading the gang leader's text as if hoping it will change. Vijay stares at the ground, his shoulders tense, while the others argue in hushed, frantic voices.

Avi: This is ridiculous. How the hell did we end up here? We came to Goa for a vacation, not to star in some gangster horror show!

Shubh: I told you. I told you this was a bad idea. But no, Bunny wanted to "explore the unexplored Goa." Now look at us—explored to death!

Bunny: Oh, come on. How was I supposed to know this place came with complimentary gangsters?!

Avi: Oh, I don't know, Bunny. Maybe because every sane person just stays at the beach and drinks with the Russians? But you wanted "authentic Goa." Well, congratulations! You found it. Now we're authentically screwed!

Bunny: (angrily) Hey! All I wanted was a little fun. You're acting like this is all my fault!

Shubh: Oh, I don't know. Maybe it's because IT IS YOUR FAULT?! If we'd stayed in the room or on the beach like normal people, none of this would've happened!

Bunny: Yeah, sure. Let's all blame Bunny. Forget the fact that Vijay stabbed a guy, or that Maya dragged us into this psycho gang war—

Maya: (cutting him off, coldly) Don't you dare put this on me.

Bunny falls silent under Maya's icy glare. Avi turns to Vijay, his frustration boiling over.

Avi: And you! What the hell were you thinking, picking a fight with gangsters?! What are you, some kind of action hero?

Vijay: I was trying to help her.

Avi: (sarcastic) Oh, great! Well, mission accomplished, Vijay. She's dead, and now we're next.

Bunny: Fantastic pep talk, Avi. Really inspiring.

Maya: Maybe the gang leader's right. Maybe handing Vijay over is the only way to survive.

Everyone freezes, staring at Maya.

Vijay: You can't be serious.

Maya: You killed his brother, Vijay! Do you think they'll just let us walk away because you're sorry?

Avi: She has a point. This whole mess is because of you. Maybe you should face the consequences.

Bunny: Are you both insane?! Vijay saved that girl! He was trying to do the right thing!

Shubh: And now we're all going to die because of it!

The group spirals into overlapping arguments, their voices rising until Vijay finally shouts, silencing them all.

Vijay: Enough!

Vijay looks at each of them, his face a mixture of anger and desperation.

Vijay: I didn't want this. Any of it. But if giving myself up is the only way to save you... fine. I'll do it.

Bunny: (grabbing Vijay's arm) No way. We stick together, no matter what.

Maya: This isn't about loyalty, Bunny! It's about survival!

Bunny: You think he's the problem? Look around, Maya! You dragged us into this mess with your sister's secrets!

Maya lunges at Bunny, her face twisted with anger.

Maya: Don't you dare talk about her! You have no idea what she went through!

Vijay pulls Maya away, stepping between them.

Vijay: (firmly) Stop it. Both of you. We don't have time for this.

As the argument cools, Bunny notices something odd: faint smoke rising from behind the shack.

Bunny: (pointing) Look. They've got a fire going back there.

Maya: Probably signaling the rest of their men.

Avi: Great. Reinforcements. Because this wasn't bad enough already.

Vijay: Or... they're distracted.

The group turns to him, confused.

Vijay: If they're focused on regrouping, that gives us a chance to hit them first.

Shubh: You want to attack them?! Have you completely lost your mind?

Vijay: It's the only way. If we wait, they'll come for us, and we won't stand a chance.

Maya: He's right. We can't outrun them forever.

Bunny: Okay, fine. But can we try not to murder anyone this time? I'm running out of excuses for my therapist.

The group creeps toward the shack, sticking to the shadows. Maya and Vijay lead the way, with Bunny and Avi flanking them and Shubh reluctantly bringing up the rear.

Outside the shack, two gang members are standing guard, smoking and chatting in Konkani.

Gang Member 1: "kityaka phaka amakam itali vata palovachi padata jenna ami tankam khanyachyaya khinaka marunka shakatata. jashem te jumvya thavana paluna vachunka shakanata karana hem sagalem udakana vyapillem asa ani puraya jumvo over lidarachya malakicho ashillyana boti nata." ("Why the fuck we have to wait so much when we can kill them at any moment. As they can't run away from the island as this all is covered with water and there is no boats as the complete island is owned by over leader.")

Gang Member 2: "amachya phudaryaka khelapaka avadata. jashem tumi sangalam ki tankam hangachyana khanyacha vachunka melana. dekhuna, taka apalo goda vela kaduna hya chale ani chalayeka marapacho asa." ("Our leader likes to play. As you said that they can't go anywhere from here. So, he wants to take his sweet time to kill these boys and the girl.")

Maya signals for silence, motioning for Bunny and Vijay to flank the guards.

Bunny: (whispering to Vijay) You do the stabbing. I'll do the moral support.

Vijay: (deadpan) Thanks. Super helpful.

The group's ambush starts with surprising efficiency: Vijay tackles one guard, disarming him and knocking him unconscious with a rock, while Bunny smashes the other guard in the face with a thick log, shattering his nose. But their victory is short-lived as the commotion draws attention from inside the shack.

The door bursts open, and gang members pour out, guns raised. Maya barely has time to shout a warning before bullets start flying.

Gang Leader: (yelling in Konkani) "hya madarachodyanka dhara" ("Capture these motherfuckers")

The group scrambles for cover as the gang fires wildly into the night. Shubh trips and falls into a puddle of mud—or what he thinks is mud—until the metallic smell hits him.

Shubh: (gagging) Is this... blood? Oh my God, it's blood! I'm sitting on someone's insides!

Bunny: At least it's warm, right? Small comforts.

Shubh screams and scrambles to his feet, slipping again and accidentally knocking a corpse into a nearby gangster's legs. The gangster stumbles, firing his gun into the air.

Maya fires her stolen gun, grazing one gangster's arm. The man howls in pain, clutching his wound, but continues charging toward them. Vijay grabs a jagged metal pipe from the ground and swings it at the gangster's head, connecting with a sickening crack. Blood sprays across Vijay's face as the man collapses in a heap.

Bunny: (wincing) Uh, Vijay? You've got something... (gesturing to his face) everywhere.

Vijay: (panting) Shut up and grab a weapon!

Maya ducks behind a tree, reloading her gun as another gangster charges at her with a machete. She waits until the last second, then side steps, tripping the man into a pile of flaming debris from the shack's growing fire. His screams echo as the flames engulf him.

Shubh: (watching in horror) Did... did his eyeballs just pop?

Bunny: Yep. That's going in the therapy notes.

Bunny picks up a stray machete but immediately fumbles it, sending it spinning through the air. It lands blade-first in the foot of a charging gangster, pinning him to the ground.

Gangster: (screaming in Konkani) "hamva tuka maratam... hamva... aahhh!!!"("I'll kill you... I'll... ahhh!")

Bunny: Hey, uh, thanks for standing still!

The gangster tries to pull the machete free, but Bunny panics and grabs a nearby frying pan from a pile of junk. He swings it wildly, smashing the gangster in the head with a loud clang.

Bunny: Oh no, he's still twitching! Do I hit him again? Is that the rule?!

Maya: (shouting) Just keep moving!

Meanwhile, the fire Bunny accidentally started spreads quickly. Flames lick at the walls of the shack, causing cans of oil and ammunition inside to ignite with loud explosions. Shrapnel flies everywhere, and a piece of jagged metal embeds itself in a gangster's shoulder.

Gang Member: (screaming) " devam khatira tuka maratalom hamva tuka maratalom!!!" ("I will kill you for god's sake i will kill you!!!")

He collapses, blood pooling beneath him as Bunny shouts from behind a tree.

Bunny: (yelling) Hey, tell God I said sorry, okay?

The exploding shack sends more gangsters running, but one stubbornly charges toward Avi, who stands frozen in terror.

Avi: (yelling) Oh God, oh God, oh God—

Vijay tackles the gangster just as he raises his knife, pinning him to the ground. Vijay's fist connects with the man's face repeatedly until blood spatters his hands, his knuckles raw. Maya pulls Vijay back before he can land another hit.

Maya: (firmly) Enough. He's done.

Vijay: (breathing heavily) Not until they stop coming.

A particularly large gangster grabs Shubh by the collar, lifting him off the ground. Shubh flails wildly, his hand landing on a broken bottle. With a panicked scream, he stabs the bottle into the gangster's eye. The man drops Shubh, clutching his face as blood spurts everywhere.

Shubh: (hyperventilating) Oh my God, oh my God, I killed him. I'm a killer now. I'm gonna go to jail.

Bunny: (patting his back) Don't worry, Shubh. You'll have great street cred.

Shubh faints, landing face-first in another puddle of blood.

The gang leader steps out of the shack, unharmed despite the chaos around him. Flames illuminate his scarred face as he surveys the carnage. His men are either dead, injured, or fleeing, but his calm smirk remains.

Gang Leader: Impressive. You little rats have claws.

Maya raises her gun and fires at him, but he ducks behind a burning beam, the bullet grazing his arm. He reemerges, holding a knife dripping with blood—his own or someone else's, it's unclear.

Gang Leader: (grinning) But claws aren't enough to kill a snake.

He whistles sharply, and more footsteps echo from the jungle as reinforcements arrive.

Maya: (shouting) Run!

The group scrambles away as the flames consume the shack entirely, collapsing the structure with a deafening roar.

CHAPTER TEN

THE RECKONING

The group sprints through the dense forest, their breaths ragged. The fire from the shack still lights up the sky behind them, and the gang leader's reinforcements are closing in.

Shubh: (panting) I can't keep running! My lungs feel like they're on fire!

Bunny: Oh, great! Maybe they'll let us stop for tea if we ask nicely. Keep moving!

Maya, clutching her injured shoulder, stumbles but pushes forward. Vijay helps her, his face set in grim determination.

Maya: We can't outrun them forever. They know this terrain better than we do.

Avi: Fantastic. So what do we do? Send them a strongly worded letter?

The group pauses briefly at the edge of a ravine, their options running out.

Maya: (looking around) There's a cave system nearby. My sister and I used it once to escape them.

Vijay: (nodding) Lead the way.

The group enters the cave, the air damp and suffocating. The faint sound of water dripping echoes eerily, and the darkness presses in on them. Bunny pulls out his phone for light, the dim glow casting long shadows on the jagged walls.

Shubh: This place is straight out of a horror movie. Next thing you know, we'll be eaten by cave monsters.

Bunny: Don't worry, Shubh. If anyone gets eaten, it'll probably be you. You look the most delicious.

Avi: Can we please focus?

As they move deeper into the cave, Vijay suddenly freezes, gripping his head as another memory surfaces.

The memory hits Vijay like a freight train, vivid and unavoidable:

"The memory hit Vijay like a tidal wave. He saw the party clearly now:
neon lights flickering erratically against the backdrop of a rundown Goan shack-turned-nightclub. A thumping Konkani remix of a Bollywood hit blared through cheap speakers, mingling with the chaotic chatter of the crowd.

The scent of coconut oil and salty ocean air clung to their skin, mixing with the sharp tang of sweat and alcohol. A makeshift bar in the corner served cheap feni shots, the strong, fiery liquor burning the throats of eager tourists and locals alike.

Bunny: (in the flashback) "I don't trust a party without a DJ booth. This is sketchy as hell."

A group of Russian tourists danced in one corner, their movements erratic and wild. Near the center of the room, Maya's sister stood nervously, clutching a drink while the gang leader approached her, his voice low but threatening.

Gang Leader: (sneering in Konkani) "tumi tumachem utara kenna puraya karatale va tumakam tumachi suvata hamva dakhovanka jaya" ("When are you going to fulfill your promise or you want me to show you your place")
The girl flinched, and Bunny stepped in, his voice sharp despite

the pounding music.

Bunny: (firmly) "She's with us. Leave her alone."

The memory blurred as fists flew, bottles shattered, and the acrid smell of spilled liquor filled the air.
"

Vijay snaps back to the present, his breathing heavy.

Vijay: I remember everything.

The group stops, turning to look at him.

Maya: What happened? Tell me!

Vijay: At the party... We tried to protect her. We fought them. But... (pausing) they followed us to the cabin. They killed her.

Maya's face crumples, grief mixing with anger.

Maya: And you didn't stop them.

Vijay: We were out because of drugs till then. We were not able to do anything.

Before they can process the revelation, footsteps echo from the cave entrance.

Gang Leader: (mocking) Running into a cave? Clever. But you can't hide forever, little rats.

The group panics, their fear amplified by the confined space. Maya leads them deeper into the cave system, hoping to lose the gang.

Shubh: We're going to die here. They'll trap us like rats.

Bunny: Would you stop saying 'rats'? It's not helping!

They find a narrow crevice and squeeze through, but Maya stumbles again, her injured shoulder bleeding heavily. Vijay helps her, his face set.

Vijay: (to Maya) You're not dying here. I won't let you.

The gang corners them in a larger chamber of the cave. The flickering lights from the gang's flashlights create a chaotic, strobe-like effect as the fight begins.

Vijay: Using a stalactite as a weapon, he takes down one gangster with brutal efficiency, blood spraying across the cave walls.

Maya: Despite her injury, she fights fiercely, stabbing one gangster in the leg with a sharp rock.
Bunny: In a moment he grabs a fallen flashlight and bashes a gangster's head in, only for the light to flicker wildly.

Shubh Accidentally trips a gangster into a pool of water, where he flails and hits his head on a rock, sinking beneath the surface.
The gang leader and his men close in, the fight descending into chaos. Blood stains the walls of the cave, and the group scrambles to defend themselves.

Shubh, panicking and desperate, grabs a length of rope hanging from a rock. He swings it wildly, his eyes squeezed shut.
Shubh: (screaming) Get away! Get away!
The rope catches a loose stalactite, dislodging it with a sharp crack. The rock crashes down onto a gangster, knocking him out cold. The sudden impact sends another gangster stumbling backward into a pool of water, where his head strikes a jagged rock with a sickening crunch.
The cave falls silent for a moment as everyone stares at Shubh, who stands frozen, holding the rope.
Bunny: (grinning) Well, Shubh, I take it back—you do have killer instincts.
Shubh: (stammering) I—I didn't mean to! I was just... swinging it...

Vijay: (patting his shoulder) Doesn't matter. You saved us.

Shubh looks down at the fallen gangsters, his face pale but his chest rising with the faintest hint of pride.

The gang leader steps forward, calm and menacing, as the last of his men fall.

Gang Leader: (sneering) So, it's down to us.

The gang leader pulls out his knife, circling the group.

The gang leader stepped forward, his machete catching the faint moonlight, a menacing grin spread across his scarred face. He swung the blade lazily, the sound slicing through the tense silence.

Gang Leader: (mocking) "You've caused me enough trouble. Time to end this."

Maya moved to the front, her face hard with determination.

Maya: (to the group) "Run. I'll hold him off."

Vijay: (grabbing her arm) "No! We're not leaving you!"

Maya: "You have to. This is my fight. They won't stop until one of us is dead."

Before Vijay could argue, the gang leader lunged at Maya, his machete slicing through the air. Maya dodged, narrowly avoiding the blade, and swung a broken wooden plank she'd grabbed from the ground. The makeshift weapon glanced off the gang leader's arm, but he barely flinched, his grin widening.

Gang Leader: (grinning) "Feisty. Let's see how long that lasts."

Maya tried to keep her distance, using the plank to deflect the gang leader's strikes, but his speed and strength overwhelmed her. With a swift move, he batted the plank out of her hands and grabbed her wrist, twisting her arm behind her back. Maya cried out in pain as he pulled her closer, his blade hovering near her throat.

Gang Leader: "You've got guts, I'll give you that. But this ends here."

The rest of the group stood frozen, panic written across their faces.

Bunny: "What do we do? He's going to kill her!"

Vijay: (desperately) "We have to distract him!"

Avi grabbed a heavy rock from the ground, his knuckles white as he gripped it tightly.

Avi: (to Shubh) "You circle behind him. I'll distract the bastard."

Shubh nodded, crouching low as he moved carefully to the side. Avi took a deep breath and hurled the rock with all his strength. It struck the gang leader squarely on the shoulder, making him stumble backward and loosen his grip on Maya.

Gang Leader: (roaring in pain) "You little punks! You're dead!"

Taking advantage of the moment, Shubh rushed forward and grabbed Maya's arm, pulling her free from the gang leader's grasp. Maya stumbled but quickly regained her footing, stepping back to rejoin the group.

Maya: (breathing heavily) "Thanks, Shubh."

Shubh: "Don't thank me yet. He looks angrier now."

The gang leader, clutching his shoulder, glared at the group with fiery rage, ready to pounce.

Vijay: (stepping forward) "This ends now. You want us? Come and get us!"

Gang Leader: (laughing darkly) "Brave words for dead men."

Bunny: (muttering to Avi) "This is the part in every Bollywood movie where the heroes magically pull off something insane."

Avi: (smirking) "Guess we'll have to improvise."

Maya stood between Vijay and Shubh, her eyes locked on the gang leader.

Maya: "We're not running anymore."

The group tightened their formation, a mix of defiance and fear in their eyes as the gang leader raised his machete and ready to attack.

CHAPTER ELEVEN

THE LAST BLOW

The group hesitates, frozen as Maya squares off against the gang leader in the dimly lit cave. The flickering flashlight in Bunny's hand casts eerie shadows on the walls.

Maya: You think you're so untouchable, don't you?

Gang Leader: I don't think, sweetheart. I know. And soon, you'll be nothing more than a story I tell my men.

The gang leader lunges at her with his knife, and Maya parries with a sharp rock she picked up earlier. The clash of steel and stone echoes through the chamber.

Vijay steps forward, desperate to intervene, but Bunny grabs his arm.

Avi : (whispering harshly) What are you doing? She told us to run!

Vijay: (angrily) I'm not leaving her!

Shubh: (panicking) Are you both insane? If we stay, we're dead. If we leave... (pausing, looking conflicted) well, she's probably dead too, but at least we won't be!

Avi: (grimly) Shut up, Shubh. This isn't the time.

As Maya fights the gang leader, her movements grow sluggish from her injury. The gang leader smirks, sensing her weakening.

Gang Leader: (mocking) Is that all you've got? No wonder your sister didn't stand a chance.

Maya's face twists with rage, and she drives her rock into his side, drawing blood.

Maya: Don't you dare talk about her.

The gang leader stumbles back, clutching his wound, but he's far from finished. Realizing Maya won't last much longer, Vijay picks up a broken stalactite and charges.

Vijay: (yelling) You're done!

The gang leader deflects Vijay's attack, but the distraction gives Maya time to recover. Bunny, Avi, and Shubh join the fray in their own chaotic ways:

Bunny hurls his flashlight at the gang leader's face, hitting him squarely in the nose.

Avi tackles the leader from behind, only to get elbowed in the ribs and thrown off.

Shubh, in a panic, swings a loose rope around wildly, accidentally tripping himself and a nearby gangster.

The fight devolves into chaos, with grunts, screams, and the sound of fists and rocks colliding.

The gang leader gains the upper hand, slamming Maya into a wall. Blood trickles down her face as she struggles to stand. Vijay leaps onto the leader's back, driving the stalactite into his shoulder.

Gang Leader: (roaring) You little shit!

He throws Vijay off, but Maya, fueled by desperation, picks up a jagged piece of metal and plunges it into his thigh. Blood sprays onto the cave floor as the gang leader collapses to one knee, growling in pain.

Bunny: Oh God. Is that... is that bone? Can we see his bone?!

Shubh: (vomiting) I can't—I just—bleeerrgh!

The fight is pure chaos. Blood stains the jagged cave floor as the group battles the gang leader.

Maya is on the ground, gasping for air after the gang leader's brutal assault. Vijay is dazed, barely able to stand, blood dripping from a gash on his forehead.

Bunny stands frozen at first, watching as his friends struggle. His usual humor is gone, replaced by wide-eyed fear. The gang leader sneers at him, dragging himself to his feet despite his injuries. Blood pours from the wound in his thigh, but his eyes burn with rage.

Gang Leader: (mocking) You're next, clown. What are you going to do? Make me laugh to death?

Something inside Bunny snaps. He glances at a jagged piece of metal lying nearby, picks it up with trembling hands, and steps forward.

Bunny: (low, trembling) You think this is funny?

The gang leader smirks, taking a step toward him.

Gang Leader: (mocking) Oh, I think it's hilarious. Look at you. Shaking like a leaf. You don't have the guts.

Bunny suddenly lunges, driving the jagged metal into the gang leader's chest. The man stumbles, his eyes widening in shock, but Bunny doesn't stop. He pushes the gang leader against the cave wall and twists the metal deeper, his face eerily calm.

Bunny: (darkly) You know what's funny? I was supposed to be the guy who made everything lighter. The fun one. The joke guy. (pausing) But you? You made me realize something.

The gang leader gurgles, blood bubbling at his lips as he struggles to respond.

Bunny: (leaning in close) Life's not a joke. It's a goddamn horror show. And guess what? (whispering) I just became the punchline.

With one final push, Bunny yanks the metal out. The gang leader collapses, blood pooling around him as his body twitches once before going still.

The cave falls silent except for Bunny's ragged breathing. The others stare at him in stunned disbelief.

Avi: (softly) Bunny...

Shubh: (wide-eyed) Oh my God.

Bunny drops the bloodied metal and turns to the group, his expression blank.

Bunny: (coldly) What? You thought I was just going to let him kill us?

He walks past them to help Maya to her feet, his hands still shaking but steady enough to pull her up.

Maya: You... saved us.

Bunny: (bitterly) Yeah, I'm a real hero. Let's get out of here before his friends show up.

As the group tries to catch their breath, Maya's phone buzzes. She pulls it out with trembling hands, her face darkening as she reads the message aloud:

Maya: (reading) "Nice try. You think killing me ends this? Look behind you."

The group spins around just as a shadow emerges from the deeper part of the cave. A figure steps forward, wearing a bloodied mask and holding a machete.

Shubh: (whispering) Oh no. No, no, no.

The masked figure raises the machete, and he swings it at the group.

CHAPTER TWELVE

A VEIL OF VENGEANCE

The group froze as the masked figure emerged from the shadows, his bloodied machete dragging along the rocky floor. His labored breathing echoed in the cave, amplified by the oppressive silence.

Bunny: (clutching his jagged metal weapon) "I don't know about you guys, but I vote we skip introductions and start running."

Shubh: (whispering) "Please tell me that's a ghost."

Avi: (grimly) "Worse. It's real."

The figure stopped just a few feet away, tilting his head as if studying them. Then, with deliberate slowness, he removed his mask, revealing a face eerily similar to the gang leader's, save for the deep scar slicing across his jaw.

Masked Figure: "You killed him. My brother. And now you're all going to pay."

The gang tensed as he stepped into the flickering light of the burning shack outside, his machete gleaming.

Younger Brother: (mocking) "You think you can walk into our world, kill my brother, and just leave? You've humiliated us. And in our world, humiliation is paid for in blood."

He paced slowly, gesturing with the machete, his voice growing darker.

Younger Brother: "We aren't just some gang. We are Goa's shadows. The streets, the cops, the politicians—they all kneel before us. And now you'll kneel too, before you die."

Bunny: (nervously, raising his hands) "Okay, okay, how about we skip the kneeling and maybe... just let us go? No hard feelings?"

The brother smirked coldly, shaking his head.

Younger Brother: (chillingly) "You're already dead. You just don't know it yet."

He raised his machete, pointing it directly at Maya, who stood weakened but defiant.

Maya: (spitting blood) "You're all the same. Cowards hiding behind your gangs and weapons."

The brother's smirk vanished. With a growl, he lunged at her, machete slicing through the air.

Vijay intercepted him just in time, grabbing the machete with his bare hands. Blood dripped onto the rocky floor as the blade sliced into his palms, but he refused to let go.

Vijay: (gritting his teeth) "Not today!"

The two men struggled, their grunts echoing off the walls. Bunny seized the opportunity to swing his jagged metal weapon, slashing the brother's arm and drawing a deep, bloody gash.

Bunny: (yelling) "Take that, you psycho!"

The brother roared in fury, backhanding Bunny with enough force to send him sprawling to the ground.

Avi: (grabbing a rock) "Hey, over here, you scar-faced maniac!"

He hurled the rock with all his strength, hitting the brother squarely in the face. Blood spattered from his nose as he stumbled, disoriented.

Younger Brother: (snarling) "You'll regret that!"

As the brother charged at Avi, Shubh, trembling but determined, swung a wooden plank at the back of his knees. The brother fell to the ground with a howl, his machete skittering across the floor.

Maya, despite her injuries, crawled toward the machete. Her fingers closed around the hilt just as the brother lunged for her. With a yell, she stabbed the blade into his thigh, the steel sinking deep.

Maya: (through gritted teeth) "You don't scare me."

The brother howled in pain, blood pooling beneath him. Bunny and Avi rushed forward, their weapons raised.

Bunny: (grinning) "Let's finish this, boys!"

Bunny swung his jagged metal weapon again, this time slicing across the brother's shoulder, the sound of tearing flesh sickeningly loud. Avi followed with another rock, smashing it into the brother's temple.

The brother, bloodied and staggering, refused to fall. He grabbed a knife from his boot and lunged at Vijay, slashing wildly. Vijay dodged the blade, then tackled him to the ground.

Vijay: (yelling) "Shubh, now!"

Shubh, mustering all his courage, picked up a heavy lantern and smashed it over the brother's head. The glass shattered, and flames erupted, catching onto the brother's clothes.

Younger Brother: (screaming) "You'll all burn with me!"

As the flames spread, Bunny grabbed the machete from Maya and delivered a final blow, slashing across the brother's chest. The man's screams faded as he collapsed to the ground, motionless.

The fire roared, consuming the cave. Smoke filled the air, choking them as they scrambled for the exit.

Maya: (weakly) "We have to go... now!"

Bunny and Vijay helped Maya to her feet, while Avi and Shubh cleared a path through the debris. They stumbled out of the cave, coughing and bloodied, as dawn broke on the horizon.

Shubh: (collapsing onto the ground) "I swear... I'm never leaving Yamunanagar again. Ever."

Bunny: (panting) "Yeah, because Yamunanagar is so much safer than this."

Maya: (weakly) "Don't celebrate yet. The rest of the gang will come looking for him—and us."

The group exchanged weary glances, the weight of the night etched into their faces.

Vijay: (firmly) "Then we keep moving. Together."

The group trudged into the jungle, battered but alive, leaving the burning cave and the nightmare behind them—for now.

CHAPTER THIRTEEN

THE END OF THE NIGHT

The group emerges from the jungle, stumbling onto a secluded shoreline as the first rays of dawn streak across the sky. Their clothes are torn, their bodies covered in blood and dirt, but the sight of a small, abandoned boat tied to a weathered dock sparks a glimmer of hope.

Shubh: (collapsing onto the sand) I swear, if I ever see another tree, I'll set it on fire.

Bunny: Well, good news—there's a boat. And it's not made of wood.

Maya: (weakly) It'll have to do. Let's go.

They climb into the boat, with Vijay and Avi fumbling to untie it. The group works silently, the weight of the night heavy on their minds. As they drift into open water, the sounds of the jungle fade, replaced by the gentle lap of waves against the hull.

The boat takes them back to Goa, where they finally dock at Palolem Beach. The vibrant hues of the sunrise clash starkly with their bloodied, disheveled state. Bunny looks around, his face lighting up as he spots a familiar sign.

Bunny: (grinning) The German Bakery! It's still here!

Avi: (staring at him) You've got to be kidding me.

Bunny: What? After all that, I deserve carbs.

Without waiting, Bunny leads them to the bakery, where the smell of fresh bread and coffee fills the air. They sit at a corner table, drawing a few curious glances from other patrons. Bunny immediately orders a huge breakfast spread.

Shubh: How can you eat after... everything?

Bunny: (chewing) Easy. Step one: don't think about the gangsters we crushed with rocks. Step two: focus on the fact that these croissants are amazing.

Avi: (shaking his head) You're a psychopath.

Bunny: (grinning darkly) Says the guy who didn't flinch when that gangster's eyeball popped out.

The table falls silent, the humor giving way to the weight of what they've survived.

After breakfast, The group walks along the soft sands of Palolem Beach, their feet dragging as the events of the past night weigh on them. The golden sunrise paints the sky with streaks of pink and orange, a serene contrast to the chaos they survived.

Maya stops abruptly, turning to face the others.

Maya: (softly) This is where I leave you.

Shubh: What? You're staying here? Alone?

Maya: (nodding) Someone has to clean up this mess. And I need to do it for her—for my sister.

The group falls silent. Even Bunny, for once, doesn't have a joke.

Avi: You don't owe anyone anything, Maya. You could come with us. Start fresh.

Maya:This is my fresh start. Staying here, making sure they don't hurt anyone else—it's the only way I can honor her.

She looks at each of them, her expression softening.

Maya: You all saved my life. I'll never forget that.

Her gaze lingers on Vijay, and the others quietly step away, giving them space. Vijay shuffles his feet, looking anywhere but at her.

Maya: You're a terrible liar, you know that?

Vijay: What?

Maya: Back in the cabin, when you said you didn't know how we ended up there. Your face gives you away.

Vijay chuckles awkwardly, rubbing the back of his neck.

Vijay:I didn't know what else to say.

Maya steps closer, her tone softening.

Maya: You're a good man, Vijay. My sister... she would've liked you.

Vijay's throat tightens as he struggles to respond.

Vijay: (guilty) I didn't do enough to save her.

Maya: You did more than most would. You tried. That's more than anyone else ever did for her.

She reaches into her pocket and pulls out a small silver bracelet, tarnished but still gleaming faintly. She presses it into Vijay's hand.

Maya: (whispering) This was hers. For luck. You're going to need it.

Vijay looks at the bracelet, then back at her, his eyes stinging.

Vijay: What about you?

Maya: (smiling sadly) I'll make my own luck.

She leans in and kisses his cheek before turning and walking away. The rising sun silhouettes her as she disappears into the distance, leaving Vijay standing alone with the bracelet clutched in his hand.

Bunny: (from behind) You okay, Romeo?

Vijay turns to see the others watching him. He exhales, nodding.

Vijay: Let's go home.

Back in Bangalore

Days later, The group sits in Vijay's apartment, a quiet lull settling over the room. The TV hums faintly in the background, playing a random action movie none of them are watching. Shubh stares at his hands, while Bunny leans back, cracking jokes that barely mask his unease.

Shubh: (breaking the silence) So... we almost died. Multiple times.

Avi: Yeah. Great vacation.

Bunny: (grinning) Are you kidding? Best trip ever. We should do it again sometime.

Shubh: NEVER.

Shubh: I can still hear it, you know? The screaming. The gunshots.

Bunny: Don't forget the part where I threw a flashlight at someone. Pretty sure that's what saved us.

Avi: Yeah, Bunny, the flashlight was the hero. Not Maya, not Vijay. Definitely the flashlight.

Bunny: C'mon, guys. How often do you get to crush gangsters with rocks and set things on fire? It's character-building.

Avi: You need therapy.

Bunny: (leaning back) Yeah, probably.

Their laughter fades into a comfortable silence, a shared acknowledgment that they've survived something they'll never forget.

They chuckle weakly, but the laughter fades quickly. Vijay sits apart from them, staring at the bracelet Maya gave him, the weight of the night still fresh in his mind. His phone buzzes on the coffee table, breaking the silence.

Shubh: (groaning) Who's texting you this early?

Vijay picks up the phone, expecting some routine notification. Instead, his blood runs cold. The screen displays a single message:

Unknown Number: "You left something behind at the cabin. Should I return it?"

Vijay's heart pounds as he stares at the message. The room feels heavier, the air stifling.

Bunny: (noticing Vijay's reaction) What's wrong?

Vijay: It's them.

He shows the message to the others. Shubh gasps audibly, and Avi's jaw tightens.

Avi: (angrily) This has to be a joke. Who else would have your number?

Shubh: What if... what if they're outside? What if they followed us back?!

Bunny: Calm down, Shubh. If they were outside, we'd be dead already.

The tension thickens as Vijay stands and moves to the window, looking out into the dimly lit alley below. At first, it seems empty. But then, in the shadows, something moves—a figure steps back into the darkness, their face obscured.

He received one more message:

"You thought it was over? It's not. We're watching."